The Days Between the Years

INSPIRED BY A TRUE STORY

SHERRY AUSTIN

The Overmountain Press

JOHNSON CITY, TENNESSEE

ISBN-10: 1-57072-324-9
ISBN-13: 978-1-57072-324-7
Copyright © 2007 by Sherry Austin
All Rights Reserved
Printed in the United States of America

1 2 3 4 5 6 7 8 9 0

In memory of Sergeant Willie Hubert Owens, II ("Uncle Junior")
—of many, one.

ACKNOWLEDGMENTS

I am grateful to: Dr. Donna L. Halper, author and broadcast historian, for her invaluable expertise about the early days of radio and television; Michael Uys and Lexy Lovell, coproducers of *Riding the Rails,* an award-winning documentary film about the hobo culture of the Depression era; Errol Lincoln Uys, author of *Riding the Rails: Teenagers on the Move During the Great Depression*, the companion book to the film; Anne Osborne and Charlene Pace, editors of *Saluda, North Carolina: 100 YEARS—1881–1981,* for background information about that special little mountain town where I based my story; Joe Nickell, author of *Secrets of the Sideshows,* a book about the history and culture of carnival curiosities; Fred Chappell, author of *I Am One of You Forever,* for his tall tales featuring Southern literature's most human hound dogs, which inspired the dogs in these pages; Oma Owens Moore, whose true story of a love transcending time inspired this story, which I've needed to tell for so, so long; and all those of the World War II generation—those on the home front as well as on the front lines—whose sacrifices made possible the foundation all our present freedoms and comforts are built upon.

Letters

Mrs. Trixie Goforth, getting on up in years and just lately starting to feel like it, slipped out of bed one December morning, itching to weasel her way out of the mental straightjacket her three adult children had strong-armed her into. She stepped down the hall and into the kitchen of her little brick ranch house with its green-striped awnings in Spindale, North Carolina, where she'd lived for fifty years. And where she'd live until she dropped! She let her children know it, too, every time they started up again about hauling her off to the Methodist Home.

She nosed through the cabinets like a nervy little mouse, wondering how in the world she could forget where she put the coffee canister, which she used every single morning. The way she misplaced things lately unnerved her something awful, especially after she'd had just the teensiest memory lapse back in the summer and her kids had gotten their bowels all in an uproar and started threatening her with incarceration.

She found the coffee, finally—practically right in front of her face! In a few minutes the Mr. Coffee choked and sputtered like somebody had it by the throat, and the rich smell of strong coffee brewing and of peppery sausage sizzling in the iron skillet damped down the firestorm in her head—for the moment. She parted her kitchen curtains and peeped out at the gray December light and thought that maybe, just maybe, a dusting of snow on her holly and nandina bushes would calm her nerves and give her some of the Christmas spirit, of which she possessed not so much as one ounce. The right kind of spirit, she hoped. She'd already had enough visitations from the other side lately, thank you very much.

She wrapped her robe tighter around her and decided not to think about it, knowing she ought not to let her mind dwell on such mysteries so early in the morning, when dimness still filled every corner of her small house and cobwebs still hung in the corners of her mind. She hustled to pour herself a cup of hot coffee. The last of the liquid dripped from the Mr. Coffee and sizzled when it landed on the warmer. She took a quick sip and stepped over to the kitchen table, where, along with a roll of stamps and sheets of Christmas Seals, a stack of Christmas cards lay, unsigned and unaddressed.

How awful that so close to Christmas she hadn't bothered to write the first card! She put on her bifocals and ran her finger over the names on the list, half of them people who'd sent her cards last year, which obligated her to send them cards back. But she had a good mind not to bother with it. She was too old for all that nonsense. And postage was so high. And besides, all those cards that people sent slowed down the postal system, which she figured was why she hadn't received a Christmas card yet from Esther. That and the fact that she had known of Esther to write cards and letters and mislay them so they sometimes never even got mailed at all.

Dear, sweet, lovely Esther. Esther Purvis was one of her last close connections to the war days, the last still living, unless she counted Dot Clark, her first cousin who lived in Idaho, or Lettie Newsome, who was more of an acquaintance than a friend. Trixie and Esther had known each other as girls, from the time when Trixie and her great aunt Olivia, whom everybody in the family called Ollie Pearl, used to take the train into the mountains and spend Christmas in Saluda, the little town where Esther had lived. Trixie and Ollie Pearl used to stay at Laurel Terrace, an old boardinghouse owned by Ollie Pearl's sister-in-law, Edna Templeton. Esther was three years older than Trixie and had worked nearby at Pace's Store on Main Street. Whenever Trixie made a run to the store for a bottle of Syrup of Pepsin for Edna's sour stomach, Esther would slip Trixie a stick of sassafras candy for free. Oh, the memories they shared of those days!

They'd both married young, and they'd both married soldiers. They'd lost contact when Esther moved away for a few years. Then one day, at the tail end of those Howdy Doody days following the Second World War, the doorbell rang right in the middle of "The Secret Storm."

"Avon calling!" somebody chirped. Trixie opened the door to Esther's beaming face. Esther was a born Avon lady with skin like the finest milk glass, a face softly rouged like a peach. Esther lived nearby then, and Trixie bought what cosmetics she used straight from her. The two women met for coffee and gossip, baby-sat each other's kids, raised money for the March of Dimes, and worked together at the Veterans of Foreign Wars auxiliary. They got together once a week to discuss the latest trashy developments on the TV show "Peyton Place."

And then—wouldn't you just know it!—Esther's husband landed a job at Beacon Manufacturing in Swannanoa, just far enough away to curtail their visits. They vowed to keep in touch, but after a while, with both of them raising families at a time when most people had only one car per family, when most people viewed long-distance phone calls as an extravagance, they visited and talked rarely. They passed back and forth the occasional letter and Christmas card, but years slipped by, children grew up, married, divorced. Grandchildren arrived, husbands died. Time marched on with little communication between them.

But then, back in the summer—surprise, surprise!—Esther had sent Trixie a long catch-up letter, several pages written in Esther's lovely, curvy script on mauve stationery. In preparation for reading the letter, Trixie had made herself a cup of tea, placed two ginger-snaps in the saucer next to the cup, taken the phone off the hook, and cleaned her bifocals with Windex. She settled in her recliner and read the letter, running her forefinger under each word, sometimes two or three times, as if to catch some niblet of information that might have slipped between the lines. Esther told how she'd continued to sell Avon for years, continued raising money for the March of Dimes, had gone to Hawaii to see the *Arizona* Memorial, where her first husband, Teddy White, had fallen during the Japanese attack on Pearl Harbor in 1941. She told Trixie how sorry she'd been to see "The Secret Storm," their favorite daytime soap opera, end in 1974, and, by the way, did Trixie still have that fruitcake recipe she used to use, though, truth be told, she didn't look forward to Christmas anymore—hadn't it gotten so out of hand?

In that same letter she explained that she'd moved around from state to state with her son, whose job required him to transfer often, but now she'd made plans to move back home to guess where? Saluda! To Laurel Terrace Assisted Living, which a local developer had built on the site where the old boardinghouse by the same name had been razed. The same boardinghouse where Trixie, as a girl, had spent some Christmases. The very same place Trixie and her first husband, Frank, had inherited and had actually operated for a very short while, early in their marriage.

The new Laurel Terrace was barely a few years old, Esther said. Of course Trixie knew about it; she had read all about it in the newspaper. It had a little café, Esther wrote, a room with an exercise bike and a treadmill, and a place where she could get her hair fixed and her nails filed and polished. And she'd be right back in the lovely mountains she loved so well, right near her daughter, who'd recently come home to retire in nearby Tuxedo. Trixie remembered Esther's daughter as an odd woman who cared more about the stray dogs she took in than her mother, but Esther seemed happy about it, so Trixie was happy for her. Esther now lived so much closer to Trixie—and for good.

And that tickled Trixie positively pink!

"You *will* come up here and see me!" Esther had written. She expected to move sometime in late October or November, she wrote, and if Trixie couldn't find a way to visit her before the holidays—hadn't the holidays become so busy busy busy, so all about ticky-tacky!—Esther hoped she would visit after the first of the year. Trixie had wanted to write back, but Esther, as absentminded as Trixie herself lately, hadn't included a return address.

Of course, Trixie wanted to visit Esther, but, strangely, she'd found herself putting it off. She didn't want to even think about assisted living facilities, and she had not wanted to see the new Laurel Terrace in particular. The old inn was less than an hour's drive up the mountain, and Trixie used to drive by it fairly often. A time or two she had strolled along Main Street in Saluda to browse the artsy shops, visit Pace's Store, have a chili cheeseburger at Ward's Grill. She'd walked through the lovely, woodsy sanctuary of the Episcopal Church of the Transfiguration on the hill above town, but she had not done any of it for years, certainly not since they'd torn down the old Laurel Terrace Inn.

Though she had read in the paper about the new building project and its cutesy amenities, she hadn't wanted to go there since the construction had begun. She didn't want to see a squat, ugly, modern building right there where Laurel Terrace, the old boardinghouse, used to stand. The old place had stood high on the hill, as if it had sprouted and grown up with the trees. She remembered the ivy-edged stone steps that led to the broad front porch, where two coonhounds, Red and Blue, used to lie around like throw rugs. Now she'd probably see a gradual rise of ugly concrete leading up to an ugly concrete stoop. What if the builders had cut down the leggy old-growth rhododendron that had banked the front porch? What if they'd wiped out the huge wedge of mountain laurel that stood between the grounds of the house and the railroad track, and replaced it with metal maintenance sheds or an asphalt parking lot?

She took a slow sip of coffee and smiled. A path had curved lazily through those thick laurel woods in her day, with branches twisting upward toward the distant sun. Not far from the path's end, a clear amber creek slid over rusty gold and green mossy stones. Something unimaginably ancient, secretive, and mysterious always hung in the cool damp air in those woods and by that creek, something a boy she had met there had helped her see, something she couldn't put a better name to, even after the passing of many years. How she would hate to discover that the creek had filled in with silt and sludge from the construction of Laurel Terrace Assisted Living.

So she had put off going to see Esther and felt guilty about it. She'd planned to go for sure, though, when the holidays were over, after the first of the year. But then, right around Thanksgiving, she'd received yet another letter from Esther in which she mentioned having a gentleman friend. Though no one could pay Trixie to tangle herself up with a man again, they couldn't pay her not to run up to Laurel Terrace to see Esther and get the scoop on hers!

But by the time she'd received Esther's last delicious bit of news, the little episode in a gas station in Forest City had occurred. Afterward, Trixie's children had informed her that if they caught her driving anywhere but to church, the store, the beauty shop, or her primary care physician—all within two to three miles of her house—they'd have to "talk about" the Methodist Home.

"Where somebody can keep an eye on you, Mama," her son Terry Wayne had said.

"Where I'd be under twenty-four-hour surveillance, you mean!"

"For your own good," all three children agreed.

"Pooh! I'd rather go ahead and die than go where everybody spends their last days talking about their kidney stones and playing pinochle!"

Well, if she didn't send a Christmas card to another soul, she ought to send one to Esther. She picked up one of the cards and scribbled a quick note inside. She told Esther that she'd love to drive up to see her, but since her children had taken it upon themselves to be the long arm of the law, she guessed she'd have to wait until after the first of the year when one of them could take the time to drive her up there. Esther would understand. She knew all about busy, bossy kids.

Besides, Trixie already had concrete plans to defy their orders. The very next morning she would sneak off and drive up to Asheville, something she absolutely could not put off. If she got by with that transgression, she just might take to the wheel and pay Esther a visit before the holidays. And if she got by with that one, she just might drive off into the sunset all the way to Idaho to see her last living cousin, Dot, and see what her children thought about that!

"You have a Merry Christmas, now," she wrote to Esther, "and a happy New Year." The card she'd chosen had a redbird and his tawny mate standing on snow-covered spruce branches. After she signed her name, she added, snickering softly: "And how's the love life?"

Stories

My handwriting looks like chicken scrawl! Trixie thought, as she closed and addressed the envelope. She used to have pretty handwriting. She used to have a lot of things: twenty-twenty vision, get-up-and-go, a memory sharp as a tack. What a handsome card, though, as lovely as any of those cards you'd have to pay four or five dollars for at Hallmark. Whenever she saw Esther next, Trixie would tell her that she'd bought a whole box of those cards for a dollar after Christmas last year. Esther would appreciate Trixie's thriftiness, with both of them remembering the Great Depression, with both of them having lived on fixed incomes for years. She put extra Christmas Seals on the envelope to make it especially eye-catching when Esther received it.

But her heart just wasn't in writing out the rest of the cards, or in putting the electric candles in the windows, or in pressing the poinsettia tablecloth and matching napkins she would use for dinner on Christmas Day, or in putting on Bing Crosby singing "White Christmas" while she strung the lights on the tree. Or even in stirring up an extra fruitcake like she used to do at Christmas, even though no one in her family much cared for fruitcake, except for Terry Wayne, who sure didn't need it. And she wasn't about to go to the mall and wear her feet into stumps shopping, either!

All because, truth be told, though she went through the motions, she didn't care all that much for Christmas, and she had felt that way for years. Years! Everything had changed so much. Time was, Terry Wayne would borrow the church van and they'd all squeeze into it and drive down the highway to see the Christmas lights at McAdenville. Children, spouses, grandchildren, and sometimes the dog, would pack in around her like Vienna sausages. The dog did not have fresh breath, and the children would just about squeeze the breath out of her, but she didn't mind. "You got enough room, Gram?" they would ask. So sweet, so thoughtful, and so excited. But now they had ball games to go to, dates to keep. "Do we have to?" they had whined last year when she suggested they go.

Now it was a different day and age. For the longest time she'd had this nice, normal family. Then her middle child, Thomas, the dentist, up and left his near-perfect wife for his hygienist, who always came into Trixie's house looking like she smelled kerosene, and brought along her skinhead son, who sat around with a sneer tattooed on his face.

Why couldn't anything stay the same? "Mother, this looks so good!" they used to say when they sat down to eat dinner on Christmas day—a big dinner that she'd spent Christmas Eve making, proudly sparing nothing in the way of salt, sugar, and saturated fats. A meal that would draw stray dogs from a mile away and would cause her skinny new daughter-in-law to sneak into the kitchen and binge on the sly. But these days they were all health nuts, every one of them except for Terry Wayne, who still loved to eat and had a belly as round as his bowling ball to prove it, bless his heart.

How simple life was back in the 1930s with Ollie Pearl, Naomi, Edna, and the others at Laurel Terrace. Even though Trixie's first Christmas there had ended so badly, with her heart broken. Even though if she'd never gone there in the first place, she wouldn't have got herself saddled with Frank. How awful of her to think of Frank that way, her first husband, the father of her children, a veteran of that most necessary of wars. Well, she had her reasons.

But all in all, the way they had celebrated Christmas at Laurel Terrace had been simple and good. And that was back during the Great Depression, too, which proved that you could have some good times in the midst of hard times. How she'd loved the Shirley Temple paper dolls the Blackburn sisters, who boarded there at the time, had given her, even though she'd outgrown dolls by that time. But something that would have thrilled her to get back then, her grandchildren would look at like it came out of a Cracker Jack box.

Not that she was so easy for them to buy for either. Though they tried, she could count on one hand the times they'd bought her something she didn't stuff in a drawer. She had been pleased to receive a photo of the whole family one year, a copy of her favorite old black-and-white movie, *How Green Was My Valley*, the next. But just last year, they'd all gone in together and bought her a computer, of all things. At her age! Why, she was thrilled to the gills the summer day when lighting ran in on it and blew it up in a delightful spectacle of sparks and smoke! And when they'd given her a cell phone, she'd sneaked and dumped it into a sack of old clothes she planned to take to Goodwill, then told them she'd lost it.

"There's not a thing in this world I need or want," she told them whenever they needled her to find out what to buy for her. "Not anything, anyway, that can be bought."

"But, Mother—"

"If you all know where to buy back my good eyesight, my natural teeth, my get-up-and-go, then go get it. Otherwise, save your money!" she said, then slammed her lips shut like a clam.

She wouldn't think of spoiling Christmas for everybody else, so no one really knew how she felt about the time of year but Esther.

And, well, Penny at the beauty shop. Just the day before, when she'd gone to get her hair fixed, Penny, teasing more than Trixie's hair, winked at her in the mirror. "All ready for Christmas?"

"Ready as I'll ever be!" Trixie snapped.

Penny threw back her head and roared. "You tickle me!" she said.

Trixie, still at her kitchen table, took a bite of her sausage biscuit. She frowned as she swallowed it. Jimmy Dean put too much sage in his sausage for her taste, or else her taster had gone off! She wondered if she wrote Jimmy Dean a letter and complained about it, if he would write her back. He'd always seemed so easygoing on TV. She wrapped the rest of the biscuit in wax paper and put it in the icebox. Icebox! She remembered when everybody called the refrigerator the icebox. And still, lately, every once in a while, she caught herself calling the TV the radio. Well, the radio had been the center of the world in her girlhood.

She made herself drink the whole cup of coffee, thinking maybe it would give her some get-up-and-go. But, shoo! It tasted like ashes. Her taste buds and her appetite had gone or had started going, as had nearly everything and everyone she'd ever known or cared about. That was another thing not to like about the holiday season, she thought, as she forced herself to her feet and started clearing the table. The holidays were a time when memories, sweet and bitter, got stirred up too much to suit her.

Looking out the window as she finished washing up her breakfast dishes in the sink, watching snowbirds alight and cluster in the bare limbs of the red maple tree at the road, she recalled the unusual circumstances that had stirred up her latest stew of memories. She recalled the day back in October when she kept looking out the same window with great anticipation until a refurbished 1960s van wobbled into her drive. A young man and woman, documentary filmmakers, one with a camera, the other with a notebook, came to the door intending to film her talking about her life during the Depression and World War II. She had expected them, of course. They had reached her through the local chapter of the VFW, where she had done volunteer work with the auxiliary. The pair saw Trixie— the widow of not only one, but two veterans of the war—as a good candidate. They had written her a letter explaining that they were doing a documentary film, called *The Days Between the Years,* about women on the home front during the war.

Those of you who lived through the Great Depression and the Second World War, the letter said, *could leave no greater legacy than to share the way your times changed your lives.* She knew they wanted to interview her in a hurry because her generation was fading fast. All those scratched-out names in her address book showed it, all the cards and letters she didn't get anymore. It was awfully crowded now, that dark side of her memory.

The morning before the film crew came, she had fussed with her hair until the effort made her arms tired and sore. She'd wished Esther could come and fix her face up and polish her nails. What if she got camera shy and tongue-tied? She guessed she could talk about the same things she did when one of her grandchildren had interviewed her for a school project called "Tell Us About the War, Grandma." She'd told how the whole earth shifted on its axis on December 7, 1941, in small ways— how she'd had to make her ice tea without a speck of sugar because the government rationed it, how the food shortage had forced her to think of umpteen ways to cook Spam—and in ways too deep for words.

But how should she act in front of the camera? She had not a single role to her credit since she'd played Aunt Eller that time the church ladies put on a hurry-up and hokey little production of

"Oklahoma!" And now, suddenly, she had a starring role, in a *motion picture* that people could watch over and over! Worn out from all the fussing around, she had plopped her scrawny bottom at her vanity and stared into the mirror. She tried to draw her eyebrows to look like Rita Hayworth's. She smeared some plum-colored rouge onto her cheeks and wondered if eating all those prunes all those years was what had made her end up looking like one.

Elijah, the boy setting up the camera and tripod, looked like a bean pole, his T-shirt stretched tight across a sunken chest, his jeans hanging from his hip bones. She'd fix him a double-decker pimento cheese sandwich and make him eat it before he left. The girl, Skye, who said she'd ask the questions, looked pretty well fed. She had sharp, listening eyes behind Coke-bottle eyeglasses. The three of them sat out on the patio. The yellowing vine twining around the wrought iron, with the dogwoods turning purple-red all around, would make a nice backdrop on film, they said.

"I don't like complaining about having to use ration coupons for sugar and doing without nylon hose when so many people at that time truly suffered," Trixie had told Skye as they warmed up a bit before the camera rolled. What sacrifices she had made were too small to mention, she said. After all, she'd not lost her life or her liberty. She'd had two husbands, both veterans, and both had come back alive and uninjured after the war.

But Skye assured her they wanted precisely those kinds of memories—her memories of the days between her years—the everyday ways people's lives had changed because of the war, the small sacrifices and, most of all, the sudden turns that sent ordinary people down roads of no return.

Roads of no return. Something welled up in Trixie when she heard those words.

Skye leaned over, her elbows on her knees, and looked deep into Trixie's eyes. "Let the heroes of battles and the survivors of concentration camps tell their stories, Mrs. Goforth. We want you to tell yours."

At first Trixie stared out at the camera bug-eyed and kept fingering her hair.

"Why don't you start by telling us a little bit about the Depression years as you remember them, Mrs. Goforth," Skye prodded.

The Depression? How did you even start to describe something like that? "Well," she began, "it seems that to people these days, depression is something you can pop a pill for, but for the Great Depression, there was no easy fix. . . ."

She could run out the film, she said, but she'd still need to make another whole movie to tell all the little stories, the little indignities. You had people, the young and the old, the wise and the half-wits, wandering the streets, riding the rails, homeless, begging. Many people felt lucky to get a "knee-shaker," what the hoboes called a handout on a plate you had to balance on your knees. "And I'm talking about real people," she said. "Americans!" One face in particular came to mind.

"What were the Depression years like for you, personally, Mrs. Goforth?"

Those days had been tough she said, but not as tough for her as for others. Though she was just an eleven-year-old girl when her young mother ran off with a harvest tramp, Trixie was rescued by her great aunt Ollie Pearl in a matter of days. The worst thing was how in that day and time people would brand a child for what her mother had done; they'd watch her all her life to see if she followed suit so everybody could have the satisfaction of saying "the apple doesn't fall too far from the tree." A different day, a different time.

But her cup had run over, compared to so many others, especially after Ollie Pearl had rescued her back in the '30s. Still, all these years later, she sometimes felt like an abandoned child, as if everyone else in the world had gone on a picnic to the lake. But a lot of people had felt that way then, she knew. In that way, if in no other, she had plenty of company.

The more Trixie talked, the more the smallest details from her past floated to the surface, then remained unsinkable as Ivory soap. And to think, most days now she couldn't even remember if she'd taken her high-blood-pressure medication! Indeed, the world had changed on December 7, 1941, in big ways written up in the history books, and in countless little ways most people would never know.

She told how she'd done the good and honorable thing and married a soldier boy, Frank Templeton, who would become the father of her children. She told how she'd kept the home fires burning while her husband played his role in the Pacific theater. She told how she learned to "use it up, wear it out, make it do, or do without," how she'd worked making parachutes, as one of millions of women who tended the jobs of absent soldiers. She told how, after the taste of independence and financial freedom, she'd felt a new kind of discontent when the war ended and the men returned to their jobs and she, like other women, returned to the house. She'd played Rosie the Riveter during the war, only to get hustled right back to playing Betty Crocker once the war was over, stuck in the house all day long with Mr. Clean.

After Frank came home from the war, Trixie had three children like stairsteps. Frank died in '71, and some years later, she'd married Buck Goforth. Frank and Buck, her two veterans.

"Come on," Trixie told Elijah and Skye. "I'll show them to you."

Pictures

Elijah and Skye followed Trixie inside to the wall of pictures in the hallway, where, right next to the thermostat, hung a picture of Jesus kneeling on a rock in Gethsemane, praying for his cup to pass from him, begging for a stay of execution. Around the picture, other photos and mementos in frames of every size and shape covered the wall like wallpaper. She wouldn't have anybody know it, but every once in a while she would stop there when she adjusted the thermostat and look at the pictures of the ones who had passed on. She couldn't hold their faces in her mind, which brought on a loneliness that only looking at their pictures or small tokens of memory could ease for a while. She pointed out Frank's and Buck's dog tags and medals that she had mounted and framed, buttons from the uniform Frank's father wore in World War I, Civil War coins that had belonged to Aunt Ollie Pearl's grandfather.

But pictures took up most of the wall. Not just family pictures, either: Eleanor Roosevelt standing in front of a Christmas tree with the children of the unemployed at a Trade Union League party, tiny school pictures of grandchildren of long-dead friends. She thought of someone's picture she'd give her right arm to have, no matter how old and faded.

The pretty lady with the surprised look on her face, she told them, was her friend Esther Purvis, the one with whom she shared so many wartime memories. The bird-faced woman with no chin and a turkey neck was her great aunt Ollie Pearl. "The one who saved me," she said, then gave them a short rundown of how she was orphaned and how Ollie Pearl had rescued her. *The one who, along with the rest of society, weaseled me into marrying Frank,* she thought but didn't say. Ollie Pearl had been all wrapped up in the times she lived in. Hadn't everyone?

And there was Edna Templeton, who ended up her mother-in-law. "The one with the face like a hatchet and a disposition to match it!" she said.

Elijah and Skye looked at each other and grinned.

Trixie tried to pass over the picture of Frank and pointed to one of Buck. That was her second husband, Buck Goforth. Yes, right there, the one who looked like a bulldog in overalls.

But Skye pointed to a picture of Frank and said, only half teasing, "That's Clark Gable, right?"

No, she said, that was Frank, her first husband and the father of her three children. Right there was another picture of him, in his sailor's uniform. She'd married him quick as a lick before she was even eighteen years old, the way so many girls did in those days. Oh, she didn't want to think about it for a while.

"You all must be hungry." Trixie practically shoved them into the kitchen, where she made the three of them some pimento cheese sandwiches—a double decker and extra mayo for Elijah—and ice tea.

Elijah filmed the whole thing, the three of them eating at the kitchen table. He claimed he was stuffed after he ate half his sandwich, but she guilted him into eating the rest of it. She was well-warmed to her subject by then and talking up a storm. She was starting to look forward to the film when they finished it. Maybe they'd host a premiere and she'd arrive to cameras clicking and flashbulbs popping like she was a star in the golden years of Hollywood.

"Well," she said when, to her disappointment, Elijah wound the interview back around to her first husband, "when Frank came home in '45, he used the GI bill and went to technical college, then he did pretty well with his auto parts store." What she didn't say was that later Frank had all but lost his shirt gambling, that they had quickly lost the inn at Laurel Terrace, which they had inherited from his mother, and that they made ends meet mainly because Ollie Pearl had left them her small house, which Trixie had the good sense to rent out for extra income.

She could have told them half a dozen irritating things about Frank—like how he was a mama's boy—but instead she told how he loved the Jack Benny show, first on radio and then on TV, how he was partial to five-flavor pound cake, how he had built a backyard playground set for the children, how he and the boys loved to fix up antique motors and exhibit them at the fair.

"Sounds like a good husband, a good father," Skye said, unsure of it, prodding.

"Oh, he was a good father," she said. *Give the devil his due.*

She didn't tell them that more than Frank's eye roved over the years, and how she didn't leave because women of her generation just didn't do that. And no matter what, Frank was a veteran of what historians already called, rightly or wrongly, "the good war."

"Now, Buck, my second husband, he was a pistol," she said. He was the proprietor of Hawg Heaven Barbecue and could work circles around men half his size. Heaven, to him, was happy customers, a Grade-A rating, his truck washed and waxed, his grass cut, and himself splayed out on the couch with the TV tuned in to a twenty-four-hour "Bonanza" marathon.

Buck had survived the war and a quadruple bypass but had died less than a year after they married. He'd slammed his ram-tough

Dodge truck into a utility pole and died on the spot. They'd been married barely long enough for him to give her his name.

What she didn't say was that she'd seen Buck along about dusk one day last summer, out in the backyard on his lawn tractor, mowing, waving to her to come outside the way he used to do when he wanted to show her something. How like a little boy Buck could act, always wanting her to come out and look at something he'd found—a baby rabbit in the irises, a snake he'd mowed over, or a nest of yellow jackets. Busy in the kitchen, she'd wave him off to say she'd come out and look at it later. But that time she couldn't bring herself to wave him away; she couldn't bring herself to go out there to him either. A little chill had come over her at the thought, so she just wiped her hands on her apron and watched him and watched him until he melted away in the twilight, tractor and all. He'd been dead for years then. She hadn't told a soul that she'd seen him. She'd learned to keep that kind of thing to herself.

When they finished with the interview, Trixie felt exhausted but renewed at the same time. For the past year or so, she'd felt herself coming unraveled, body and soul, like a skein of yarn pawed by a crazy cat, but now, even though she'd dredged up all those memories, she felt as if she'd plugged her soul into a colossal cosmic socket. To think that after she was gone, future generations might watch *The Days Between the Years* and hear how she, Mrs. Trixie Goforth, had sold war bonds, rolled bandages, grown her Victory garden! How she'd done what was before her to do and made a fine job of it, thank you very much. She was only one of many, though, and she'd want the whole world to know it.

"This is all really wonderful, Mrs. Goforth," Skye said. "Truly wonderful, but. . . ."

"But what?"

"I think you have a story you haven't told us yet."

Trixie looked at the young woman, saying nothing for a long moment. "Well, there's a little story, I guess, not that it would mean a thing to anybody but me."

"That's what we want, Mrs. Goforth—the little stories." Skye placed her fist right under her heart. "Little stories that come from deep down in here. May we come back, say, after the first of the year, and talk again?"

And now here it was two months later, with the second interview coming up soon after Christmas had passed. As Trixie thought of how she would tell her story, memories started flowing like water from a spigot. She felt tired after she washed up the breakfast dishes. It had been a while since she'd swallowed the last of the hot coffee; now she felt chilly. When she shuffled down the hallway to turn up the thermostat, she straightened up the picture of Jesus. She looked at him kneeling almost prostrate on the Gethsemane rock, his hair falling down around his shoulders in lustrous auburn waves, his upturned face awash in a wedge of heavenly light, as he prayed for his cup to pass from him.

A Little Incident

The following afternoon, in willful violation of her children's orders, Trixie headed up the mountain toward Asheville. When she slipped into the left lane and passed a great big diesel truck, the driver scowled down at her like a hawk from its perch. As if he owned both lanes! When she swerved in front of him—with at least two car lengths to spare, she thought—he laid down on his horn, and in her rearview mirror she could see his mouth working as he made an ugly gesture with the middle finger of his hand.

Ill-mannered! Well, let him rant and rave. Let *him* have the heart attack, the stroke, the aneurism. She had her own worries.

Her chief worry was that her three children would somehow find out she was flying up I-26 like a bat out of hell. And on an overcast day in December with the temperature hovering at thirty-two degrees, when only a little rain could fast-coat the highway with a sheet of ice. But they wouldn't have to worry, so long as they didn't know, would they? And how would they know? She didn't have that cell phone, which she had cunningly lost, so they couldn't ring her up and catch her on the road. If she had a wreck, they'd surely find out, though, so she'd best take extra care. She looked down at her speedometer, at the little needle inching up, inching up. What if the highway patrol chased her down and issued her a speeding ticket? It wouldn't be the first time they'd stopped her for speeding, and Terry Wayne might find out about it since he'd been a policeman for a while and had cronies in all areas of law enforcement. Now that she thought about it, he might have paid some of them under the table to keep an eye out for her. Better not attract attention. She lightened her foot a bit and slowed down to a sensible five miles per hour over the speed limit.

Of course, no one actually knew what she was up to. Unless . . . unless she'd slipped up and told Penny at the beauty shop! Had she? Something about lying backwards with her sudsy head in a sink loosened up her tongue at both ends. For all she knew, she had told Penny. For all she knew, Terry Wayne or her daughter, Lou Ann, had paid Penny under the table, too. To monitor her every move!

But she'd never been prone to conspiracy theories. Buck had believed everything was a sinister plot, from the Kennedy assassination to the moon walk, but not Trixie. She tried to relax, remembering she'd delivered her children a simple, believable lie that, barring an accident or speeding ticket, ought to cover her tracks. She'd told Lou Ann and Terry Wayne she was going to the doctor; that much was true, but she'd lied and said she was going to the internist three miles from her house just for a check-up, when in fact she was going to a specialist in Asheville, a good hour and ten minutes away.

"Why didn't you ask one of us to take you, Mama?" Terry Wayne would say if he found out she'd driven that far by herself. He'd flail his arms around like he was sinking in quicksand. "You know any one of us'll jump through hoops to take you anywhere you want to go!"

Well, she didn't want anybody jumping through any hoops, for one thing. And for another thing, she hadn't told them because she didn't want them to know she had an appointment with a specialist at Western Carolina Pulmonary Critical Care. With her history, knowing she had to see a specialist would have sent them all into spasms of worry. If any bad news came out of the visit, she'd have to tell them eventually, but she might as well wait until after the holidays. Why drop a pall over them in what most people saw as the season of good cheer? Sneaking off and driving herself was the sensible solution.

But she wouldn't have had to sneak if she hadn't become confused last August on her way to take a pie to a sick cousin of Buck's in Frog Level. She'd stopped at a filling station and forgot how to get home. She had sat in the car next to the pump for a good ten minutes, sweat trickling out of her hair, trying to remember, making a fumbled mess of an old map. She'd never needed a map to get home from Frog Level!

A mechanic was working on a pickup truck in the station garage, looking headless and spooky with his head and half his torso under the hood. She slapped the horn with the palm of her hand and then laid down on the horn with all the strength she had. The man's head—thank goodness he had one!—popped out from underneath the hood. He dropped his wrench and ran toward her car, bowlegged and lurching like a chimp. He stuck his head inside the window, and she grabbed his grimy, grease-monkey hands, squeezing them hard, giving him such a look that he didn't even ask her what was wrong; he just asked for her identification and when, confused, she didn't offer it, he politely reached into her purse, pulled out her wallet, and found her driver's license. He ran back to the shop and called the police, who contacted Terry Wayne, who arrived forty-five minutes later, red-faced, waving his arms like an orchestra conductor.

The episode had shaken up Terry Wayne so much that when he got her home he wouldn't let it drop.

"Now, Terry Wayne, you're making far too much of this little incident."

"LITTLE INCIDENT?" he boomed. That boy could bray like

a mule! He had her by the arm, but she pulled away from him and headed for the recliner.

"That's right," she said. "It was just a one-time thing caused by the heat, my being so tired, and a little drop in my blood sugar. Just get me a glass of ice tea and two or three gingersnaps and let me lie back in the recliner for a few minutes. I'll be just fine!"

But what did he do but call Lou Ann. Then he called Thomas in Atlanta and left a message on his voice mail. Within a few minutes here came Lou Ann, her face pinched as a peach pit with worry. Then Thomas called back and asked Terry Wayne if he ought to drive up from Atlanta over the weekend and see if there was anything he could do.

"Do about what?" Trixie fumed when she heard Terry Wayne tell Lou Ann what Thomas had said. "Mercy! You all are so worked up, you've got me worked up. I can't for the life of me understand why you all have got your bowels in an uproar over this! It was just that one time!"

They both looked at each other, then at Trixie, and Lou Ann said, "Things like that have happened more than once, lately, Mother."

"When? You tell me when!"

They didn't answer.

"Don't you all think if I'd had another memory lapse, *I'd* be the one to remember it!"

Lou Ann's eyes teared up. She refilled Trixie's ice tea glass. "Now, Mother," she said, "it's not so much memory lapses as little episodes of . . . disorientation."

"Oh, pooh!"

Lou Ann insisted on staying with her that night. Trixie, unnerved more by their suggestion of those so-called other incidents than by the incident earlier in the day, felt too agitated for sleep, but she went to bed so Lou Ann would. After the light in Lou Ann's room went off, Trixie waited a while then tiptoed into the kitchen to calm her nerves by reorganizing her recipe box.

She'd just tossed out three duplicate recipes for green bean casserole when a recent example of what Lou Ann had called an "episode of disorientation" edged its way into her memory. She remembered an early morning when she went out to pull the weeds from the beds of cockscombs she'd planted at the very back of the yard. There, in a swath of sunlight just out of the shade cast by the row of tall, dark Leyland cypresses, stood the old playground set Frank had built when their children were small. As she had always done, she dragged the butt end of the rake through the undergrowth, hoping to shoo away any snakes. After weeding her way through the cockscombs from one end of the row to another, she began to feel dizzy from stooping over so much. When she grabbed onto the tire swing's post to pull herself up, who would she see but little Ila peeping down at her from behind the top of the slide. Her childhood friend, Ila, with her dark stringy hair and the black horn-rimmed glasses that had made her look so old even as a little girl. Trixie hadn't seen her since childhood, and Ila had died before she reached fifty, years and years ago.

"Come on, let's play," Ila said. Her voice had always been a little deep for one so young.

Trixie stared at Ila and Ila stared at her.

"Come on."

"I can't right now." Trixie's own quivery little-girl voice from her distant childhood had scared her about as much as seeing Ila.

Ila shrugged. Trixie watched her climb the last rung of the ladder and swing one leg then the other over the top of the slide. A big shadow came up behind Trixie. Big hands took her by the shoulders.

"Who're you talking to, Mama?"

She nodded toward the slide, but Ila faded before her eyes.

"Myself," she had said to Terry Wayne, after a moment. "Just mumbling to myself." So, there was one of the episodes her children had on their minds, she guessed.

When Lou Ann woke up, she gulped a cup of coffee, kissed Trixie on the forehead, and told her she had some business in town. When she returned an hour or so later, she walked over to the recliner and presented Trixie with a small silver and white paper box, the kind jewelry came in. Tears rimmed Trixie's eyes as she held in her hands what was surely a token of apology. She hesitated before opening it, the better to savor the moment. A mother's pin studded with the birthstones of each of her three children, to match her mother's ring?

When she lifted the lid off the box, her face fell. An identity bracelet lay crumpled in the bottom with her name and the phone numbers for both Lou Ann and Terry Wayne on it.

"I picked out the most attractive one I could find, Mother," Lou Ann said quickly. She reached down for Trixie's wrist to put it on her, but Trixie jerked her hand back, folded her arms, and looked away, lips tight, tears streaming. "Dog tags!"

"I want you to wear this, Mother."

"I will not!"

"I'm afraid you're going to have to. Otherwise we'll have to start thinking of . . . other alternatives."

"Other alternatives? Like what? Sitting in the parlor of a rest home, head bobbing, with all the other old folks waiting to die?"

Lou Ann's face flickered from pity to annoyance. She reached for Trixie's hand and clasped the bracelet to her wrist.

"This might as well be a handcuff! Or one of those ID bracelets they put on corpses in the morgue!"

"We want you to wear it all the time, Mother."

"No!"

"Please."

"Oh . . . all right, then!" She supposed, after all, they could ask worse things of her, and probably would.

But she hadn't expected it so soon! Lou Ann, standing over Trixie—she had inherited Frank's height—then issued further orders. "Terry Wayne, Thomas, and I have discussed it, and we've agreed you shouldn't drive anymore."

"What do you mean?"

"Just as I said, Mother. It's not safe, for you or for others."

"What do you mean 'not safe'? I've never had a ticket—"

"Oh, no?"

"So I got a little speeding ticket coming down the Saluda grade where you have to ride the brakes to keep the speed down! Everybody flies down that mountain. They don't have any choice!"

"The last one was going *up* that mountain, Mother."

"Immaterial! I'm a safe driver and I have a safe car. Terry Wayne just had my tires rotated last week!"

"The car's not the issue, Mother. Your . . . presence of mind is. Didn't you read in the paper about the woman from Asheville who started down I-40 to Dollywood? She forgot where she was going—"

"Well, I suppose that's obvious, since she ended up in Memphis! But that was her, not me!"

"But, worse, Mother, she forgot who she was and that she was even going anywhere at all."

Trixie stared at Lou Ann, her eyes wide and her mouth open. She stared so long that Lou Ann must have thought she was having a stroke. Lou Ann crouched down and grabbed her by the shoulders. "Mother? Speak to me, Mother!"

Trixie kept it up for a while, to get the maximum effect. "All right then!" she said finally. "All right!" She shook Lou Ann off, pressed the heels of her hands on the arms of the recliner, and stood up, waving away Lou Ann's offer of help. While Lou Ann's confused face followed her movement, Trixie walked into the kitchen, found her purse where she kept it hanging on a hook in the pantry, and returned to the den. "I'd like you to drive me somewhere right now. If it suits you, of course."

Lou Ann brightened. "Well, of course it does, Mother," she said, reaching beside the sofa for her own purse, scrambling inside it for her car keys, smiling. "Of course! Anywhere you ask. Where would you like to go?"

"To the hospital."

"What?"

"You heard me," Trixie said. "Take me to the hospital. To the neonatal unit. I want to go warn all those new mothers of newborns what they can expect. I want to explain to them how they've just given birth to precious little love bundles who will grow up into great big, bossy . . . bitches!"

"Oh, Mother, this really does beat all."

"Do you think so, Lou Ann? You just wait until you get old and lose everything and everybody one by one—parents, siblings, husband! Your eyesight, your teeth!"

"I'm sorry about that, Mother, but—"

"Losing your freedom to drive is just about the last straw, don't you understand? I don't want to have to call on Delores next door or on one of you children to run me to the doctor's office or to Penny's to get my hair fixed or to covered-dish suppers at church or to see Esther. If I can't drive, I'd just as soon die!"

"You don't mean that, Mother."

"Don't you tell me what I don't mean!" Trixie sank back into the recliner, her upper lip quivering, her trembling fingers playing with the bracelet.

"Now, Mother, do you really think we're doing this for anything other than your own good?"

Trixie just looked away and sniffled.

Lou Ann paced the floor, pulling at her chin. A moment later she said, "All right, then. I'll compromise with you: First, no driving at night, at all, for any reason."

"You know I don't do that. I can't see to drive at night."

"You can drive all by yourself to church, to Ingles, to Penny's shop to get your hair done, and to Dr. Phelps's office." Trixie's primary care physician had his office in the same strip mall as the beauty shop. Both were across the street from the grocery, and the church was around the corner from all of it.

"But what if I want to go to Harris Teeter when they have chicken leg quarters on sale? Or to Esther's? What if Dr. Phelps sends me to a specialist?"

"Only to Ingles, to church, to Penny's, to Dr. Phelps. When you want to go to Harris Teeter or you have to go to any of your specialists, one of us will take you. And I'm sure Delores next door would be happy to, as well."

"It's only a few extra minutes up the road we're talking about."

"More than a few, Mother. And what would happen if you suddenly got disoriented?"

Trixie looked at her daughter as astonished as if Lou Ann had slapped her. "When have I ever been disoriented?" She leaned forward and stamped her foot. "You tell me when!"

"Oh, Mother," Lou Ann wailed and reached out to grab Trixie by her shoulders.

Trixie sat farther back into the recliner and covered her face with her hands.

Lou Ann knelt beside her, dropped her hands on Trixie's knees, and said, "We'll talk about your going to see Esther after the first of the year, Mother. I promise. And I don't want you venturing any farther than I told you. I mean it. If you get confused again, at least you won't be far from home and you'll be where people know you and can help you out. Terry Wayne and Thomas will probably fight me on this decision, but I'll fight for you on it, if you give me your word that you'll stick to the rules."

"All right, then," she said. *Over my dead body!* she thought.

"I have to trust you, Mother. Can I?"

"You know you can," Trixie said. *We'll see, we'll see.*

"If we find out we can't, we'll have to ask you for your car keys."

And so the word was spoken. But rules were made to be broken!

News

Trixie passed right by the exit that would wind through the hills to Laurel Terrace. She didn't have time to stop now, and it would be too late when she drove back by, but "soon, Esther, soon!" she said.

By the time she turned in to the parking lot at the doctor's office, the delicious, brazen thrill she'd felt at defying her daughter's orders had faded into a general dis-ease. After all, she was going to the doctor because of that tiny splotch that had shown up a year and a half earlier on her left lung, and she was afraid that she was going to walk out of the doctor's office with appointments for a slew of tests.

Doctor Phelps had found the spot in a routine X-ray. He'd thought it was just scar tissue, not uncommon in a woman her age, he said, but something they would need to watch to make sure it didn't grow or change. She'd had X-rays every three months afterward, and following every X-ray, she'd hold her breath and her heart would beat hard in anticipation of the results. When the radiologist told her that the spot had not grown or changed, she'd leave the doctor's office chattering perkily to the nurses and the receptionists. Then she'd drive to the Dairy Queen for a cone of soft ice cream—chocolate and strawberry swirl—to celebrate her reprieve.

And as the months went by and the spot didn't grow or change, she stopped getting so worked up over it. No growth. No change.

Good news. It had gone that way for quite a while, but after her last visit, it had changed, so Dr. Phelps had sent her to his specialist colleague in Asheville—just to make sure, he said.

"There's nobody any closer? In Hendersonville, say?"

"Dr. Singleton up in Asheville is the best lung man I know," Dr. Phelps had said.

She'd had to wait two weeks for an appointment. So there she was. She walked into the office and bantered nervously with the office girls about how nicely they'd decorated the Christmas tree in the waiting room. She had to wait a good twenty-five minutes for the nurse to call her in. She stepped on the scales; the nurse took her blood pressure and asked her a dozen questions. The nurse left her in the room for fifteen minutes, then came and took her to another room for the X-rays. When the nurse said "all done!" Trixie buttoned up her blouse and followed the nurse back to the examining room, where she sat forever and a day waiting, waiting some more.

Finally, Dr. Singleton knocked and came into the room. His eyes had that dark look that some of the doctors tried to hide. The bad-news look. He took her hand and introduced himself. He had a soft hand. She knew he must have felt her heart thumping in her fingers. He didn't make any small talk. He sat down and rolled his chair up very close to her.

Behind him, through the window, she could see gray drizzle falling. "I hope we don't have any ice," she said. She couldn't do without a little small talk. It eased her nerves, or it usually did.

He turned and glanced out the window. "I don't think we have to worry about it staying if it does. The ground's too warm. Did you bring anyone with you, Mrs. Goforth? Is there a family member or a friend in the waiting room?"

"No. Why?"

"Only because we have a lot of information to go over." He tried for a kind, calm, even tone, but his voice dripped doom.

The chill left her. She felt hot and sticky all over.

"I think it helps to have more than one set of ears to digest it all," he said. "Could my receptionist call someone, a friend or relative, one of your children?"

She put her hand to her throat. Her heart hammered so hard, she thought he could see it beating out of her chest. "No," she said. "And don't ask me to call anybody either. I don't want my children all worked up. If you have bad news, I want to tell them in my own good time, in my own way, after the holidays. And you know you can't send me home wondering. So go on now and let me have it. I've got a right to know."

He looked at her for a long time without blinking. "You're right, Mrs. Goforth. You do have a right to know."

Her voice was just on the edge of a quiver when she said, "And don't mince words because I'm old, either. I'm twice your age, and I've heard at least twice the bad news."

He nodded and stood up. He hung the earlier X-rays and, beside them, the ones they'd made a few minutes before. He clicked the lights on behind them. "Well, Mrs. Goforth," he began, pointing to a tiny white splotch on her lung in the first X-ray, "back in August of last year the lesion was still quite small." He pointed to the next picture and the next one. "And, as you know, until your recent visit to Dr. Phelps, there was no growth or change."

When he got to the last ones, the ones they'd just taken, he started saying words she didn't hear. She didn't need to. Anybody with eyes could see that the tiny speck on her lung had exploded into big white swirls like a category-five hurricane on the weather report. She thought of the auburn-haired Christ kneeling on the rock in the picture by the thermostat back home. *Let this cup pass from me.*

The doctor pulled up his chair and sat very close to her again, holding her hand while he talked to her for a long time. It was grayer outside now. The wind dragged through the trees in the parking lot, and rain pittered on the window behind him.

"It's bad, isn't it?" she said.

"As you can see just from these X-rays, the situation appears quite advanced."

"What do we do?"

"Well, first I'd like to conduct a biopsy just to be absolutely sure. We'll take a look at your lymph nodes. Then we'll need to take bone and brain scans to see if the tumor has metastasized and how far. We need to determine, if we can, if the malignancy is primary, or if the colon cancer you had twelve years ago is rearing its ugly head. That could help us determine treatment options."

Treatment. A little surge of hope shot up in her heart. "So there *is* something we can do?"

He hesitated. The rain hit the window harder.

"The truth," she said.

"The treatment I'm referring to is primarily palliative, to make you as comfortable as we can." He held her hand tighter to calm the little tremor in it. He watched her and waited a full minute before he went on. "But we can always fight, Mrs. Goforth, if you choose to do so. We can try to buy time. We can declare war on the cancer. We can go after it with all the ammunition we've got. But we also have to give serious thought to the quality of your life if we do that. These coming days are your days," he said. "And it will be for you to decide whether you want to spend them fighting tooth and nail for your life—or living it."

He watched her for a long time. That was the first time in her life she'd known a doctor not to hurry her out the door.

"How are we doing?" he finally asked.

"Well, I don't know how *you're* doing," she said, trying for a weak, little smile, "but I don't feel like I've just won the lottery."

He took both of her hands in his. She watched his face through the mist that had come over her eyes, the fog that clouded her bifocals. She felt sorry for this young man who could be her son. What an awful thing to have to give news like this day after day.

"Will you let me call one of your children now?"

She shook her head.

He glanced at her chart again. "You live in Spindale? That's not a short drive."

"I'll be all right," she said, "as long as I get back before dark."

"I don't like giving news like this, Mrs. Goforth. Especially with no one here with you. It goes against everything I believe in."

"I know you don't." She reached for his hand and patted it gently. "I hardly gave you any choice."

"My nurse will arrange the tests and set you up with my colleague in oncology. It's usually hard to schedule appointments so near the holidays, but we'll see what we can do. The sooner we have all the facts, the better."

"No," she said. "Not before the holidays. My children don't want me driving so far from home; I got by with it this time, but I'd really have to pull the wool over their eyes to do it again and again. I'd have to get one of them to drive me up here, you see, and I don't want them to know yet. I won't spoil Christmas for my children and grandchildren. I won't do it, so don't ask it of me. Besides, will a few more weeks make that much difference?"

He didn't answer. He wrote some things on the chart. "We'll

make an appointment for after the first of the year, then." He put his pen back in his pocket and said, "I've given you a lot to ponder, Mrs. Goforth. A lot will go through your mind, and you'll have many issues to go over with your family. I can't make any of that any easier for you, but what I can do is assure you that we have some wonderful new medications, so don't worry about pain and discomfort. When the time is right, we'll get hospice involved, and we'll do everything within our power to keep you in your home, comfortable, with your loved ones around you."

"How long do you think I have?"

He let out a long sigh.

Again, she felt worse for him than she did for herself. "I have a right to know that, too, don't I?"

"I'm not God, Mrs. Goforth, and I don't believe in making those projections, but I'm positive of one thing: You do have some time. That's all you or I or any of us have, isn't it, *some time*? Maybe time to visit a place you've always wanted to see, to visit old friends, make amends, relive pleasant memories. It's up to all of us, isn't it, to squeeze whatever we can out of every moment we have?"

In the lobby of the doctor's office, little had changed. A woman handed the receptionist her insurance card with one hand and held on to a small child with the other. A little Christmas snow globe sat on the edge of the reception desk. The little girl picked it up, turned it upside down and right side up again. She watched the snow fall over a miniature family poised to skate on an oval of mirror meant to suggest an icy pond. Somehow, Trixie navigated her body through the unreal blur of other people in the hallways. "About ready for Christmas?" somebody asked somebody else.

"Who's ever really ready?" the other voice asked and laughed.

Signs and Wonders

The walk from the shiny steel-and-glass doctor's building to her car seemed long. The rain pelted Trixie's London Fog jacket and beaded up on her sprayed hair. She'd have just enough time to make it home ahead of the dark. We all have time, the doctor had said. Some time. But how much? Six months, a year, two years, five?

When she approached the Saluda exit, she had to hold her hands fast to the steering wheel to keep from exiting. Laurel Terrace was quite a way down the winding mountain roads, and if she took the time to drive there and visit Esther, she'd be way past dark getting home. Seeing Esther would comfort her, though. Women of their age could tell each other their troubles in a way they couldn't tell their children. In the privacy of Esther's room she might bring on those tears she kept holding back, but no, that wasn't such a good idea. No need to upset Esther. She watched the Saluda exit diminish in her rearview mirror. She pictured Esther, always sparkling Esther, powdering her face and putting on lipstick, getting ready for dinner with her gentleman friend.

Trixie thought of the Laurel Terrace of long ago, of the cook, Naomi, standing by the sink of the kitchen in the old house. Naomi's kitchen was always warm and fragrant with woodsmoke and vanilla. The big windows with lots of small panes of wavy glass stretched the entire width of the broad room and looked out on the woodshed, the spruce tree, the magical laurel woods with the creek running green and golden on the other side. And the railroad tracks beyond the creek. Even the railroad tracks seemed sacred in her memory now.

On the drive home through the cold drizzle, she turned over each of several scenes in her life as if it were a vignette enclosed in a glass dome like the one the child had toyed with in the doctor's office, had turned upside down and right side up to watch the snow fall on it. Eight decades of memories—the births and marriages of children, deaths of friends, deaths of two husbands; the moment under the tent at Frank's graveside in the veterans' cemetery, and later at Buck's, when men in uniform took the flag that had draped the casket, folded it into a neat thick triangle, and placed it reverently in her hands; the day Terry Wayne had left for Viet Nam, and the day, praise be, that he came back.

But after all those memories had settled in her mind like the snow in one of those glass domes, a far earlier one kept swirling and swirling. And to think it had all taken place along the laurel ridges and by the railroad track just the other side of the mountain she had passed by only a few minutes earlier. A memory over seventy years old stirred in her mind, a memory of a boy whose path she had crossed, a boy she had known no more than a few days. What she would give to know what had ever become of him.

Trixie was about to play a silly, yet dangerous little game, she knew. She might as well be tinkering with that Ouija board somebody gave one of the grandkids one Christmas. Under normal circumstances, she avoided anything that smacked of the supernatural, the unexplained, the unknown.

That's why she'd become so upset a few weeks earlier when she drove by the house that had belonged to Ollie Pearl. Soon after Frank came back from the war, he went to technical college and bought his auto parts store in Rutherfordton. He and Trixie moved nearby to the house in Spindale, where she now lived. She wanted to look after Ollie Pearl, who'd practically raised her, so Ollie Pearl sold her house in Five Forks and moved to a little house not far from Trixie and Frank. Ollie Pearl lived in that house until she died. Trixie had a habit of driving by every now and then to see if the people she had rented it to had kept up the yard. Whenever she didn't see cars in the drive or in the detached garage at the back of the house, she liked to sneak up on the porch, peep through the cracks in the curtains, and see if they'd made a mess of the inside.

That particular time she was driving home after Senior Citizens Bingo, where she'd heard talk that the woman renting Ollie Pearl's old house liked to entertain men there—Ollie Pearl's place a cathouse!—something Trixie would put a stop to in a minute if she could prove it. So, on her way home she turned and crept down the dusky street toward the house. She saw no cars in the driveway. Three days of newspapers had piled up in the yard. Mail pushed the lid out from the mailbox. Except for the tiniest light from a lamp in the front bedroom, the house was dark inside. Trixie tiptoed up the steps to the front porch, not knowing exactly what she was looking for, but looking forward to getting her eyes full of whatever there was to see.

She had walked halfway up the steps when the front door of the house swung inward with slow, sure motion. Who stood behind the door? Her woman tenant? A man? Her woman tenant and a man? What would Trixie say to them?

She was about to turn tail and leave, when Ollie Pearl poked her head out from behind the door, looking sweet as a tea cake in matching nightgown and slippers, hair neat as a pin in short finger waves. Ollie Pearl cracked the screen door open and said, "It's about time you came in, Trixie. Can't you see it's almost dark?"

Trixie had felt as if someone behind her had a feather and was teasing the back of her neck with it. No, she hadn't completely welcomed the visions she'd had lately. And she'd never gone out of her way to dabble in necromancy, but. . . .

Trixie eased herself down on the floor beside the Christmas tree and spread the lights onto the carpet. She'd always plugged them in to make sure they worked before she strung them around the tree. But ever since her first sickness twelve years earlier, Trixie had used the little ritual as a sign. She knew it was silly, so silly, but if the lights came on when she plugged them in, she took it as a sign that she would live another year. And if one day they didn't, well, therein lay the danger in this act. But so far every year they'd come to light without a hitch.

The big cone-shaped lights were in a tangled mess, as usual. The paint had chipped off half of the bulbs. No wonder—she'd had those lights ever since nineteen sixty-something. But the kids all thought they were tacky, and last year Thomas had bought her two sets of new ones that had what he called classic, elegant, tiny white lights. They were practical, too. "If one light goes out, the rest stay on!"

"Oh, pooh!" she'd said. New technology seldom impressed Trixie Goforth. She'd tucked the new lights away in the bottom drawer of the bureau of her spare room, where she snuck all the gifts they'd given her she knew she'd never use—fancy tablecloths, rolls of scented drawer liners, the little ceramic Santa with holes in his beard for growing alfalfa sprouts.

Would the old lights work this year? Her heart fluttered a little as she untangled the last knot. She hesitated for just a minute before she shoved the crooked plug into the wall socket and. . . . Yes! They lit up in candy colors—red, green, yellow, orange, blue—all over her tasteful beige carpet. She thought they'd never looked brighter. Well, good! She unplugged them, then stood up on her step stool and spent a good hour stringing the old, faithful lights around the tree.

She was down on her hands and knees by the tree, holding the last length of the strand in her trembling hands, ready to drape the lights across the lower branches, when the kitchen door slammed. She nearly jumped out of her skin! Footsteps: *Clunk. Clunk. Clunk.* Who could it be? All the kids knew she kept a key outside in a seam under the patio awning, but they usually knocked before they came in.

"Gram?"

Thank the Lord! It was Kara, Terry Wayne's oldest girl. She stood over Trixie, big earrings dangling, tall as a pole with those platform shoes on. Trixie had never seen her in shoes like that before.

"I didn't think you were here, Gram. I knocked and knocked before I came in. Didn't you hear me?"

"I didn't hear a thing. I guess I was in another world."

"Here, let me help you!" Kara knelt and started draping the lights on the lower branches. Then she started to fuss. "You ought not to get up on that ladder, Gram! You know any one of us would've done this for you!" She plugged in the lights, which lit up like a flash of fireworks.

As they stood back and looked at the tree, Trixie didn't care if the lights looked gaudy or not. That tree, at that moment, was the most glorious sight she'd ever seen, for a reason her granddaughter couldn't know. A smile spread wide across her face. A year! A full year! She might see Kara graduate from college in May and marry that young pharmacist next December, the one who looked like Elvis. A lot could happen in a year. Thomas and his first wife could get back together again; Lou Ann's son Tadpole would graduate from Isothermal Community College. . . .

"You know what, Gram?" Kara said, holding her grandmother by the arm. "When we were little, Missy, Damian, Brian, and I used to wish Mom would let us have a tree like yours instead of that old pink and gray Victorian thing we had. We used to say there was a color on your tree for every flavor of Kool-Aid, and— Oh no!"

The lights flickered off, then back on, then off again. Kara twisted the bulbs here and there, then she gave the strand a brisk shake. She unplugged them and plugged them in again. Then she did it all over one more time. Finally she stood back and folded her arms and shook her head. "Sorry, Gram, looks like they're gone this time. Oh, well! It had to happen one day didn't it? You've still got the new ones Uncle Thomas bought, don't you? Why don't you go fix us a sandwich while I take these down and put up the good ones for you?

"Gram?" Kara looked at Trixie's face, grabbed her by the shoulders, and wrapped her in her arms. "Oh, Gram!" she whispered, right in Trixie's ear. "I know how you are about your things, but you can't get upset about that old set of lights! Daddy says they're about as old as he is. They had to die on us sometime!"

"Well, I know it," Trixie said. She tried to smile. "I'm just a sentimental old fuddy-duddy, I guess."

Trixie took the new lights from the secret drawer and gave them to Kara, then went to the kitchen and tried to pull herself together. While she warmed over some cream of tomato soup and made chicken salad sandwiches, Kara unstrung the old lights and put up the new ones and then climbed up into the attic and brought down the boxes where Trixie kept her decorations.

Trixie looked in from the kitchen, wiping her hands on a dishcloth, as Kara unwrapped and hung shiny glass balls and plastic icicles from the '50s. "Look here, Gram," Kara said, and Trixie left the kitchen for the living room. "I almost forgot about this one!"

Trixie's face lit up when she saw the ornament dangling from her granddaughter's fingers.

A Discovery

That ornament, a cross between an old-time St. Nicholas figurine and the wood-spirit faces that mountain artisans carved and sold at craft fairs, had a history unlike any of the others. Trixie had owned it for almost as many years as she had lived. Kara laid it in her hand, and Trixie ran her finger across its wild, bushy eyebrows and long, curly beard. The carver of the piece had notched a complex gaze into its eyes—multiple expressions all at once—a look somehow wise, watchful, and teasing. Dust had now settled there, as well as in the lines around its furrowed brow and in the curves of its beard. It had darkened all over. The pinewood it was made from looked old; the expression on the face looked older than time.

Trixie had hung it on the tree every Christmas for decades until it had disappeared somehow or other last year. The little ones liked to play with it, so she assumed they'd lost it. She had looked through the house over and again. Privately, she had grieved a while over its loss, but then she reminded herself that however highly she valued the piece, she had not lost one of her children or grandchildren.

Oh, but she was glad to see it again! "Where'd you find it, Kara?"

"At the bottom of this box, all wrapped up in tissue paper and snuggled in a little tin. You know that closet in the spare room that Mom cleaned out for you before we left to go home last Christmas? She found it in the corner. Luke or Sam must have carried it in there and dropped it. Or Ashlee or Trevor. I guess with all the hustle and bustle, we forgot to mention it."

Trixie held up the ornament and dangled it in front of her eyes. That it would show up now, of all times! The clever, careful workmanship of the carving, the crazy mass of curlicues of the long beard amazed her all over again.

"I'm going to run over it with an old toothbrush, Gram." Kara ran to the cleaning closet and came back. She plucked the figurine from Trixie's hand and rubbed the bristles of the toothbrush into the tiny cracks of the wood. Trixie could tell from the smell in the air that Kara had sprayed the brush with Pledge. "You know, Gram, we all liked to play with it when we were kids, and now the little ones have taken it over. Last year I saw Carson and Kinsleigh fighting over it." She worked a full minute brushing the dust from the cracks. When she was done, the wood had a new glow to it. Kara put a hook on the ornament and waved it along the branches, trying to find a place to hang it.

"It goes way, way back," Trixie said.

Kara found just the right spot for the piece. She stood back and looked at it dangling from a branch two thirds of the way up the tree. The new, tiny white lights made the old eyes, freed from dust, almost twinkle. "You know, it sounds crazy to say, but it's almost like there's something alive about its eyes." She laughed. "You know what you told us one time, Gram?"

"No telling."

"You said it—a spirit or something, I guess—had been asleep for years, for centuries, in the stick of wood that ornament got carved out of."

"Did I for a fact?" Goodness, children remembered everything.

"It scared us to death at the time! And you know what else you said?"

"Oh, mercy!" Trixie said. "I'd hate to know what all I might have said through the years that you all remember!"

"You told us that when you were a little girl, about eleven or twelve years old, you wanted more than anything in the world to be a hobo."

Trixie smiled and nodded. "Well, one day you'll look back on your younger self and wonder at the dreams you once had."

After her granddaughter left, Trixie took the ornament down and held it in the palm of her hand for the longest time. The eyes, each as tiny as the eye of a needle, looked so wise, so amused, so kind, so sad, and so *alive* all at the same time. Just like the hobo boy, Joe, who had carved them out of a rough chunk of pine, a long, long time ago.

"Are you all right, Gram?" Kara had said before she left that afternoon. She had lingered in the doorway for a moment after Trixie assured her that she was fine, just fine. Trixie figured Kara must have said something to her parents when she got home because Terry Wayne called the next day, his voice tight.

When the phone rang, she was making corn bread that she would need for the dressing she'd serve with the turkey Christmas Day. She'd already melted the Crisco in the hot iron skillet, and she'd just plunged her fingers deep into the cornmeal batter, which she always liked to goosh up with her hands. She cradled the phone between her neck and shoulder and said "hello" while wiping the slimy, grainy gunk off her fingers.

"Hey, Mama." Big deep booming voice. She could just see Terry Wayne standing in his boxer shorts in his big gourmet kitchen with granite countertops. He loved to cook. He'd won the barbecue cook-off over in Tryon for five years straight. "What's going on?"

"I'm making corn bread," she said.

"Is something wrong with you? You sound different."

"Different? How?"

"Different—worried."

She had to think fast. "Well, since you asked, I'm a little worried because after all these years, I'm trying yellow cornmeal instead of white." Not a total lie, at least. "And I don't know how it will turn out. I've heard that yellow cornmeal cooks up different from white, have you ever noticed that?"

He didn't buy it. "How'd you make out at the doctor's the other day?" She had told him she was going to her internist for a regular check-up. None of her children knew she had gone all the way to Asheville for a death sentence. "What did the doctor say?"

"Oh, nothing out of the ordinary," she said. Lie number one.

"You're not trying try to hide anything from me, are you, Mama?"

"Well," she said, thinking quickly, "he got all over me about my cholesterol." That was lie number two.

Dead silence. A tense moment when she wasn't sure he'd bought it or not. "We've talked about that again and again, Mama. You've got to lay off the sausage biscuits."

"Oh, I know it." Her voice cracked. "After the holidays." Lie number three.

"Yeah, I've heard that before. Are you sure nothing else is the matter? Sounded like you were choking or something just now."

"It's just acid reflux." She cleared her throat. How easily lies came when you got on a roll!

And then he started in on that mess about taking her to look at the Methodist Home, and the conversation ended with her telling him to just hush.

When she hung up talking to Terry Wayne, the dam of her denial broke. All the tears that had stayed frozen solid inside her melted all of a sudden. She cried into the iron skillet, tears popping and sizzling in the hot, melted Crisco. Of all that she would have to face in the coming weeks and months, she most dreaded telling her children and grandchildren. How would she tell them and when?

She wiped her eyes with her apron, and, still snuffling, adjusted her bifocals to study the VFW calendar on the wall by the phone. Her eyes followed the calendar past Christmas Eve and Christmas Day. She couldn't tell the family until after Christmas, of course. Or after New Year's. Not until the holidays were well over.

Her eyes fell on January sixth, which was marked "Epiphany." Since Epiphany was, among other things, the last of the twelve days of Christmas, she figured that the day after Epiphany was the day that the holiday season was past over, by anybody's definition. She circled it and resolved that she would tell them on that day.

She walked away from the calendar, curious about Epiphany. She'd heard it mentioned from the pulpit, of course, though they'd seldom observed it seriously. *"Epiphany!"* she said. She liked the sound of the word. It comforted her, somehow. But what exactly was it, besides the last of the twelve days of Christmas?

After she put the corn bread in the oven, she walked to the parlor and took the dictionary from the shelf by the World Book Encyclopedia, licked her fingers, and flipped the pages to the "E" section. She walked over and sat in the recliner, reading aloud in the empty house, running her finger under the words, mouthing the words slowly and carefully:

"One: 'Epiphany: A Christian feast celebrating the manifestation of the divine nature of Jesus to the Gentiles as represented by the Magi.' So, that's one definition. Two: 'January 6, on which this feast is traditionally observed.' That's another, and three: 'A revelatory manifestation of a divine being.'"

But it was the fourth and last one that she took to heart. She read on: "'A sudden manifestation of the essence or meaning of something; a comprehension or perception of reality by means of a sudden intuitive realization.'"

An epiphany. Wouldn't that be a nice thing to have right there in the wintertime of her years, for what might very well be her last Christmas? Not another subscription to the large-print *Reader's Digest.* Not another box of stationery, another roll of stamps, another tablecloth, another bottle of Estée Lauder perfume. Not even another photo of the family standing in front of a forest of dark green spruces at Shoemaker's Christmas Tree farm for her picture album. An epiphany! But she didn't have the slightest idea how to begin to ask for something like that.

The Edge of Night

Christmas Eve arrived with low-hanging clouds. The thermometer on the back patio read twenty-nine degrees. Trixie turned on WLOS News 13 out of Asheville to hear what they said about the weather, and she watched a girl named Jessica prance back and forth across the map in high heels. Didn't she know walking in shoes like that would ruin her feet and back? Trixie would write her a note and warn her about it, but you couldn't tell young people a thing.

"Can we expect a white Christmas?" Jessica teased before leading into a commercial.

"No," Trixie said out loud. "I could count on one hand the times I've seen a white Christmas here."

"We'll have the complete forecast when we come back!" Jessica piped.

Trixie pressed the mute button on the remote control and went to the kitchen to start the coffee. She couldn't stand commercials the way they did them this day and time; you never knew when you'd have to hear one advertising a pill whereby a man could increase the size of his member! Why couldn't they make cute commercials the way they used to? She remembered the Norelco commercial they used to run around Christmas, the one that began with bells jingling in the background as a grinning little Santa zipped along a rolling field of snow, riding an electric razor. The kids had loved it.

She made it back to the TV just in time to see Jessica wave her hand over a broad band of white clouds. "Those of you in the North Carolina counties bordering Tennessee might have three to four inches by the wee hours on Christmas morning." No surprise there: Any snow hanging in the air always got dumped in the higher mountains. "And a good chance of a snow shower for the southern mountain counties and the foothills."

"Pooh!" Trixie wouldn't mind seeing a little snow, but she would be surprised to see a single flake fall. She turned off the TV and turned on the radio to WNCW. Since the station broadcast right out of Spindale, they were a lot closer to the situation and ought to know the score! A dusting, the announcer said. Whatever! She poured herself a cup of coffee, hoping it might give her the get-up-and-go she needed for all the cooking she had to do. She looked out the window to survey the clouds. Just before she let the curtain fall, she saw one lazy snowflake hanging in the air, then another, hesitating, as if they couldn't decide whether to fall or not. They finally ended up on the dark green leaves of the holly bushes below the window.

A movement next door caught her eye, and she heard Delores Ledbetter's door slam. She watched Delores jump in her car and rev up the engine, getting ready to back out of the driveway like there was no tomorrow. She knew what Delores was doing, too. She was running to the store the way she always did when the weather people mentioned the slightest chance of ice or snow. What in the world could she need? She had hoarded food for months in anticipation of her family's coming.

Trixie stepped over to the front door and threw it open. "Hey! Delores!"

Delores, a blur behind the frosty glass, rolled down the window. She had a scarf printed with red-berried holly wrapped over her head and ears.

"Don't you think you ought to put some chains on your tires?" Trixie covered her mouth with her hand and snickered.

"You're laughing at me now, Miss Trixie, but we've been surprised by the weather before! I have to pick up some mineral oil for Tippy. She's irregular again." Tippy was Delores's snippy little dog.

"I'll call up everybody on the prayer chain!" Trixie said. "We'll get those bowels to moving before the day's done!"

"Oh, hush, now! You need anything from Ingles? You want to go with me?"

"No, but thanks, Delores. You know I've got it covered."

Everybody knew that. Everybody knew that come Christmas Eve, Trixie had her pantry and refrigerator well-stocked with everything she needed for Christmas Day dinner, because on Christmas Eve morning she finished up most of the cooking she hadn't done ahead. Every Christmas Eve, Thomas had Christmas with his family in Atlanta. Terry Wayne and Lou Ann, who lived nearby, let Santa Claus come early in the afternoon on Christmas Eve, then took their families to their in-laws for get-togethers. That left Trixie alone Christmas Eve, all day and night, and the arrangement suited her just fine. She needed all morning of Christmas Eve to get ready for Christmas Day when all three children, all their children, and their children, came to her house. She always cooked, cleaned up the kitchen, and set the table. Then she plopped down in her recliner, played her Andy Williams Christmas album, and rested up for the next day.

She'd already made the fruitcake, though hardly any of them would touch it. She'd made the pecan pies, and Terry Wayne was bringing his sour cream coconut cake. Lou Ann would bring Impossible Pumpkin Pie, though they'd just had it for Thanksgiving. She'd told Lou Ann she didn't know how much pumpkin pie one family ought to have to take.

"You can say the same thing about turkey," Lou Ann had said. "None of us really like turkey, anyway."

True, but what would their Christmas table look like without a turkey as the centerpiece—a golden-brown, crispy-crusted, twenty-pounder sitting proudly with legs chastely tied together, not half-done, white-splotched, and all sprawled out the way it looked when Trixie was sick one year and let Lou Ann do it. And the smell of it roasting!

She hauled the raw turkey from the refrigerator and slopped it into the sink. Martha Stewart liked to soak her turkeys in brine and roast them wrapped in butter-soaked cheesecloth, but she had somebody to clean up the mess afterwards, too. Trixie plunged her hand into the cavity and yanked out the giblets. Then she scrubbed the turkey all over, especially under the arms, where she was certain salmonella lurked. Then she slathered the big bird thick with butter—pure creamery butter. She salted it down. Lots of salt. With that health kick some of the children were on lately—all but Terry Wayne, anyway—they thought salt was poison, but she didn't buy that notion. She'd never rationed her salt intake, and she hadn't died of a stroke yet, had she? She coated the turkey with pepper, too. That wasn't good for everybody's acid reflux, but that was just too bad. For the dressing, she chopped the onions and celery and two of the three hardboiled eggs and stirred them along with three pinches of sage into the crumbled corn bread she'd made a few days before. Corn bread, not bread crumbs like Thomas's new wife, who was from St. Louis, had grown up having. She saved the third boiled egg for the giblet gravy. The smell of chopped onions and sage was out of this world. She gooshed it all up with her hands and tasted it. Enough sage, already. This wasn't Jimmy Dean cooking.

She mashed sweet potatoes and dumped in brown sugar—you could never have too much brown sugar—and spread them with pecan topping and marshmallows. She drizzled the casserole with butter and fluted it around the edges. Then she ground the cranberries for relish and put minced orange peel in it. Then she put sugar in it—lots and lots of sugar; you only live once—and mounded it up in a real crystal bowl that had belonged to Ollie Pearl. Some of the grandchildren—spoiled!—were too persnickety to eat the relish, so for them she opened up a can of cranberry sauce and sliced it onto a cut-glass dish she used just for that purpose.

Of course, she'd stir up some cream of mushroom soup with a can of green beans and pour a tin of fried onion rings on top of it—what was Christmas without green bean casserole? She'd think about that tomorrow, though. She was tired, more so than usual. She rested a while, then went ahead and spread out the poinsettia tablecloth and set the table. Might as well go ahead and make the house look as nice and festive as she could; maybe it would cheer her up. Should she use the blue-and-white Currier & Ives dishes she and Frank had inherited from his mother, the ones they'd used for Christmas at the inn? No. She set the table with plain white dishes—they went with everything.

Then she stood in the kitchen, wiping up counters that she'd already wiped clean, just because she wasn't sure what to do next. The cozy dimness of her little house in winter had sometimes delighted her, especially on Christmas Eve when she anticipated everybody's coming over, but not today. She plugged in the plastic candelabras in the windows and the new tiny white lights of the Christmas tree, but still she felt as cloudy as the skies outside. She felt like she was at the edge of night. That was a soap opera she used to watch while folding laundry back in the '50s when Lou Ann, the youngest, was little. The show opened with eerie organ music. "This *is* . . . the *Edggge of Night!*" the announcer said as a dark shadow slid sideways across New York City, where on the show somebody was always miserable and the plot was always thickening. Well, that just would not do. She put on the Andy Williams Christmas album. "It's the most wonderful time of the year!" he crooned.

"That's easy for you to say, Andy," Trixie said. She sank down in her recliner, draped an afghan over her knees, and wrapped herself up in a blanket of gloom.

The Hour of Decision

Trixie fell asleep but, judging by the clock, only for a few minutes. She was tired, as always, but this particular Christmas—so soon after her death sentence—she needed something other than rest. Maybe the kids from the church would come caroling, but they wouldn't show up until late afternoon. Maybe she should make herself go to the candlelight service at the church in the evening—this was the first year they'd had it—but nighttime was hours away. She ought to get out of herself, go see somebody, do something for somebody else. But everybody she knew lived outside the boundaries the kids had drawn around her. Besides, her friends had their families with them, or they expected them soon. They had preparations to make for Christmas Day, as did Delores next door.

She could see the mailman driving up the street. Hoping to get to talk to him, she put on her coat and wrapped a kerchief over her head and hurried across her front yard. The air was so damp and raw! She thought she ought to have put something warmer over her head; she wished she had put on gloves, too.

Her other next-door neighbors, the Bissons, had gone to Disney World for the week, and Trixie had agreed to pick up their mail. By the time she approached their box, the mailman had his hand set to open it. He saw her coming and waited. He wore a cap that balanced out his head and made it look bigger. She always thought he wouldn't be a bad looking man if he had a larger, less pointed head.

He handed her two stacks of mail, the Bissons' and her own. "Merry Christmas, Mrs. Goforth!" he said.

"Same to you, Fred. You plan to finish up early today?"

"Doing my best to."

She took a quick look through her own mail. "Goodness, I didn't expect to get any cards right here on Christmas Eve."

"We've been sort of backlogged this year," Fred told her. "Lot of cards getting delivered late." He looked up at the sky. "They're saying we might get us a white one come morning."

"Pooh! Just a snow shower, I heard. Or a dusting."

"Half an inch, maybe, according to weather.com."

"Oh, why can't they make up their minds?"

"Yeah, I know it. I better get on, Mrs. Goforth. And you'd better go on back inside. Look at you shiverin'. Merry Christmas."

"Merry Christmas, Fred."

It felt good to get back inside her warm house, but she stood at the window a moment, hating to see the tail of Fred's car round the corner. She shuffled through the mail. A Christmas card from the insurance man (hooray) and another from a real estate agent. A card from her cousin Dot in Idaho, her second cousin Rufus and his wife, Lola, one from Judy and Grover Smith from the church. None had been sent at the last minute. All of the envelopes bore postmarks from several days earlier. No wonder all her children and grandchildren called it snail mail.

And then she found a card from Esther! Postmarked December fourteenth. It was similar to the one Trixie had sent her, except it had just one cardinal, a red-feathered male perched on a snow-crusted spruce branch. Inside, Esther had written, "Come soon . . . have news about old friend . . . must tell in person. . . ."

Trixie sank into a kitchen chair and fondled the card. An old friend? Whose old friend? Esther's? Or Trixie's? Or someone they could both call a friend? Trixie tapped each finger of her left hand, counting, naming the possibilities. They hardly knew the same people—and certainly not anybody they'd call a mutual friend—except maybe for Lettie Newsome, who'd been the secretary at the VFW, but what news of her would be so remarkable? Of course, she'd hate to hear Lettie had died, but somebody their age dying was hardly breaking news they'd put in the crawl at the bottom of the TV screen. And they both had known Mildred Black—she and Esther had been close at one time—but she'd died last spring. That might not stop Mildred, though. She'd turned into such an oddball in her later years, claiming she could talk to her dead husband on the phone. So the old friend Esther spoke of couldn't be Mildred Black unless . . . unless Mildred had called Esther from the other side! Now, that would be news.

And wasn't that just like Esther! She knew Trixie too well. She knew Trixie couldn't stand the suspense. And she was right, too. Why not break tradition, call Laurel Terrace, and talk to Esther? She'd beg Esther to tell her news, but would Esther give in?

"Why don't you call up Esther and talk to her a while?" Lou Ann had suggested back in November, when Esther likely had made the move to Laurel Terrace. "What is it about people of your generation who won't call long-distance?"

"Wait until you're on a fixed income, and then you'll see why," Trixie said.

"But Mother, in this century we have something called cell phones now, with long-distance plans. You can call Esther for pennies!"

"Well, those pennies add up fast!" Besides, you needed to see people's eyes when you talked to them, especially people you hadn't visited with for a long time.

"And we have a thing called e-mail, too, but you won't hear of it."

"You've got that one right."

In person, Esther had written. *This I have to tell you in person!*

"The Hour of Decision" was the name of Billy Graham's radio program that Ollie Pearl loved to listen to. *Is this my hour of decision?* Trixie thought. She looked at the clock above the stove. *No!* She didn't have anywhere near an hour to decide! "You have some time," the doctor had said, but how long? Less time than she'd ever had before, that much was for sure.

She wasted not a moment putting on the holiday outfit Lou Ann had bought for her two years back. Maybe if she wore it she'd finally get some Christmas spirit. She slipped on the slacks made of cherry-red gabardine, the white blouse (always sensible and stylish), and the forest green sweater with snowflakes embroidered on the front. She drew on her eyebrows, taking note of that new glint in her eyes, the spark of rank rebellion! She rouged her cheeks. She teased her hair a little higher at the crown than she normally did, and she sprayed it a little stiffer to weatherize it. She put on earbobs made of clusters of tiny red and green sparkling zircons Kara had given her for Christmas a few years before. She used to think they looked loud and gaudy. Now she thought they made a bold statement. On the collar of her blouse she pinned a two-inch-tall Christmas tree with rhinestones on it. Maybe she'd cheer up the old folks at Laurel Terrace. She knew she'd make Esther's day.

She hurried to the freezer and pulled out the fruitcake to take to Esther. Why not? Nobody in her family would touch it except for Terry Wayne. She slipped her best cake cutter inside the Tupperware so she could cut Esther a slice right on the spot. Oh, and a copy of the recipe! Esther had asked for it in her earlier letter. She would be impressed that Trixie had bought the fruit and nuts for her fruitcake on sale after last Christmas and had put them in the freezer. She couldn't talk to anybody else about little things like that. The two of them could go on and on about how to pinch a penny or how during the war they would paint seams along the back of their legs to make it look like they were wearing stockings. They'd find a lot to catch up on over fruitcake and coffee, not the least of which was Esther's gentleman friend. And wouldn't Esther drop her teeth when Trixie told her that she would appear in a documentary movie? Maybe Skye and Elijah would interview Esther, too. The two friends would have so much to talk about, but it would all have to wait until Esther delivered to her the promised news of an old friend.

The Great Escape

Trixie buttoned up her coat, wrapped a kerchief around her head, shoved a hat over the kerchief, and slipped on her gloves. She clutched her pocketbook in one hand and the Tupperware cake carrier with the fruitcake in it in another. She started for the door when *Bling! Bling! Bling!* went the phone. She stopped in her tracks and looked straight ahead, as if acknowledging the ringing phone would give it supernatural power.

Bling! Bling! Bling!

One of her children was calling; she just knew it. Terry Wayne probably. "Merry Christmas, Mother," he'd say if she dared pick up the phone. "Just checking on you." Then he'd want to know why she was so out of breath.

"I'm not out of breath!" she'd say breathlessly.

"Yes, you are, too."

"I am not!"

"Going somewhere, Mother?"

Bling! Bling! Bling!

She turned around and stared at the phone like it was a coiled up cobra. What if she just let it ring? Let Terry Wayne or whoever it was think she'd made a quick run to Ingles? The grocery store was only down the road and on the allowed list, wasn't it? But knowing Terry Wayne, he'd call back in five minutes and if she didn't answer again, he'd call up Delores next door and ask her to look over and see if Trixie's car was in the driveway. Then Delores would call him back and report Trixie gone. Then, knowing him, he'd call the police to issue an all points bulletin: "Apprehend and detain Mrs. Trixie Hogan Templeton Goforth, believed to be heading west on Highway 74. . . ." She'd be five miles down the highway and here would come sirens and flashing lights swarming at her like she was that fugitive on the TV show some years back. Well, just let him! With her lead foot and some luck, she'd have crossed the Polk County line by then! But every minute counted.

Bling! Bling! Bling!

She went out the door and locked it behind her, when who would drive up but Delores, back from the store! "Where are you off to?" Delores would ask if she caught sight of Trixie. And what could Trixie say but that she was making a run to Ingles. "But I just asked you if you needed anything!" Delores would say. "Are you all right, Trixie?" she'd ask, sizing up Trixie's flushed face. She'd notice Trixie's sneaky look. Then Delores would look at her with eagle eyes. "Are you *sure* that's where you're going?"

Trixie stooped behind the holly bush until Delores pulled back into her carport. Trixie watched her take her groceries in through the side door of her house. Delores held open the door and asked her constipated little Chihuahua, Tippy, if she wanted to go out and pee pee. Trixie held her breath, waiting for Tippy to charge out the door, hightail it over to her, sniff her down, and blow her cover with that nerve-grating *yip! yip!* yippy bark. Thankfully, Tippy declined and Delores shut the door.

Trixie made a mad dash to the car, desperate to get out of her drive and down the street while Delores was preoccupied putting up her groceries and before she had a chance to look out her front bay window to see who was going up and down their little-traveled side street. Delores spent half her days doing that—and when she wasn't looking, Tippy sat on the back of the sofa at the window doing her spying for her!

With her hands locked on the steering wheel, Trixie backed out of her driveway. In her rearview mirror she could see Tippy in the bay window, watching her car, jumping up and down on the sofa back, barking her fool head off! She put the pedal to the metal to get around the corner before Delores had a chance to run over to the window and look out.

She drove through her subdivision, past all the doors with wreaths on them, past the mailboxes draped with garland, past houses covered in those twinkly icicle lights. A lot of people had them turned on, too, because it was so gloomy outside. Once out of her neighborhood, she crept down the road south of town, five miles below the speed limit. She waved to Officer Brad Gilroy, who sat in his squad car at the intersection of 221 and 74 near Forest City having his coffee and ham biscuit, both of them knowing that when she made it past the reach of his radar she'd take off like a scalded dog, and she did.

And once she got a few miles down the highway, it was smooth sailing, like a plane airborne after a bumpy takeoff. She loved the feeling of escape, of going somewhere, of going anywhere, of the pavement slipping away under the wheels of the car. That's just how Hobo Joe, how all the hoboes, must have felt with the railroad ties clicking away under the wheels of the train, knowing, if they didn't know a thing else, that something new and unexpected awaited them around the bend.

How strange that she remembered Hobo Joe so well. She'd spent such a short time with him, just a few hours stolen over no more than a few days. And over seventy years ago! Odd the hold they could have on your memory, the ones who had slipped through your life fast and early, the faces that by rights ought to get crowded out of your memory by all the ones who came after.

So, with the road stretched out before her, with the clouds hanging in low lumpy patches over the blue denim hills westward ahead of her, the words from *How Green Was My Valley* came to mind. "Strange that the mind will forget so much of what only this moment has passed and yet hold clear and bright the memory of what happened years ago, of men and women long since dead. . . ."

The Secret Storm

Esther had liked to watch the soap opera named "The Secret Storm," and so had Trixie, back when their kids were coming up. And that was what Trixie's life was like years before, back in 1935, when she was eleven years old. A man working the peach harvest came to their door asking Trixie's young mother for a glass of water and got asked in for a whole lot more. Trixie's life was never the same afterward. On the outside, her face was plain and calm as a knot on a pine log. But all the time, her insides carried on like those waves crashing against the rocky coast in the opening scene of "The Secret Storm."

After her flighty young mother had left her alone for two days, leaving her to eat stale biscuits she found in the bread box and wild green onions she pulled up from the yard, her great aunt Ollie Pearl found her sitting on the front porch, face cupped in her hands.

Ollie Pearl had wanted to take Trixie over when she was just a toddler, but her husband, Jarvis, hadn't wanted a child to raise. But Jarvis had died in 1934, so Ollie Pearl said she was going to see to it that Trixie went to finishing school to gain a patina of sophistication. She'd see to it that Trixie kept her grades up, that she took a secretarial course someday, learned bookkeeping and stenography, then married a nice man with a good steady job so she wouldn't have to use any of it. And, the most important thing, Ollie Pearl would make sure Trixie minded her morals to prove she wasn't cut from the same bolt of cloth as her mother. She warned Trixie she'd hear "the apple doesn't fall far from the tree" almost as much as "brother, can you spare a dime?" That part seemed to mean a lot to Ollie Pearl, which was why Trixie was so sorry she gave her such an almighty shock that Christmas of 1935.

Ollie Pearl always used a saucer with her coffee cup and made Trixie eat her fried chicken with a fork. She sent Trixie to Miss Martha's finishing school, but after three weeks Miss Martha said teaching Trixie was like teaching a cat to fly, so Ollie Pearl let her quit. She tried to teach Trixie social graces at home, but some little devil in Trixie made her want to wipe her nose with the palm of her hand right before she shook the hand of one of Ollie Pearl's high-nosed lady friends.

"Trixie, please don't say 'fork me another chicken shank,'" Ollie Pearl would say at dinnertime. "Say 'may I have some more chicken, please?'"

"Now, Trixie," she said after they'd had the new minister, Reverend Frazier, over for Sunday dinner, "we have right words and wrong words as regards the body functions. And if we absolutely cannot avoid passing stomach gas, we don't make a point of drawing attention to it; and we never, under any circumstances, see humor in it."

As soon as school was out for Christmas vacation, Trixie and Ollie Pearl took that first fateful train trip up the mountain to Saluda to stay a while with Edna Templeton and her son, Frank Junior, at their big boardinghouse called Laurel Terrace. Trixie looked out the window at the blur of bare trees as the train began to move faster, but she tried to pay attention to Ollie Pearl as she explained her connection to those people. Edna was the sister of Ollie Pearl's late husband, Jarvis, whom Ollie Pearl met while staying there one summer. Though Ollie Pearl had been "talking to" another man staying at the inn at the time, Jarvis had swept her right off her feet. They had married and moved down the mountain but still took the train back up to Laurel Terrace every Christmas until Jarvis passed away last year. They also spent several weeks in the summer there, as many people did. The mountain inns and train travel had depended on each other, and times were good for both until more and more people could afford automobiles. Then vacationers could gad about as they pleased and didn't care to take the train and be stuck one place for weeks anymore. Because of the automobile, train travel and the inn industry had begun to flounder. The Templetons, like many of the owners of once-prosperous inns in the mountains, had no choice but to take in long-term boarders.

The boardinghouse business was hard, Ollie Pearl told Trixie, especially in hard times, so she should prepare herself to help out. "Edna doesn't have the help she used to, except for Naomi, who's just the cook, and Naomi's husband, Rafe, the handyman. Once in a while she has a local girl, Hissy, come in and do some ironing, but that's it."

Edna had three sons, but the two oldest had grown up and gone to West Virginia to work in the coal mines. So she had only Frank Junior living with her, plus Effie and Dovie Blackburn, two sisters who had lost their homes to foreclosure, and Old Jack, who had retired from the Southern Railway and had boarded with Edna for years. And a gentleman, a veteran of the Great War, whom they all called the Colonel. Ollie Pearl mentioned the Colonel almost as an afterthought, though something in her manner suggested he might be the one she most wanted to see. He was the man she had been "talking to" when she met Jarvis, Trixie would figure out later.

On the train ride up the mountain, Trixie pressed her nose flat against the glass to get a good look at a cluster of tents and tar-paper shacks along the way. "Those are what they call 'hobo jungles,'" Ollie Pearl whispered, as if speaking of cockroaches. She took her handkerchief and made quick hard circles to wipe up Trixie's nose smears from the glass. "Whatever you do, don't do that to Edna's windows!

"And don't rip and run through the house," she said a while later when the train slowed to a halt in Saluda. "Edna won't put up with that for a minute. And mind your table manners. And be nice to Frank Junior. He was young when his father died."

When Trixie took her first step off the Carolina Special, Saluda looked to her like a little toy railroad town with toy houses set here and there along the hills. She walked up the street a ways and peeked through the windows of Thompson's Store and Pace's Store, where dim lights glowed warmly over stalls of cabbages and winter squash, rows of jars with green pickled things, red and golden jellies.

Edna had sent Rafe to pick up Trixie and Ollie Pearl in an old Plymouth, and they drove the winding way through thick hemlocks to the old place. Distance-wise, Trixie would later discover, it was a lot quicker to get to town on foot through the woods than by the curving roadways.

Mountain laurel banked the front porch of the inn and grew dark green and leathery in the woods all around. Red and Blue—one a red tick coonhound, according to Rafe, the other a blue tick—trotted from behind the house to greet them. "Shush!" Rafe said, before they had a chance to bark. Trixie and Ollie Pearl walked up the stone steps, into the hallway, and then into the parlor with its high ceiling and walls the color of parchment paper. It smelled like old wood, furniture wax, tobacco, and woodsmoke. She smelled something good cooking in the kitchen, a beef roast, onions, and potatoes, maybe.

Somebody banged away at the piano like they hadn't known how to play for long. That was Dovie Blackburn, Ollie Pearl said.

She knew Dovie from the old days. Dovie and her late husband had owned a dry-goods store in town.

Trixie and Ollie Pearl rounded the corner from the hallway to the parlor, and Dovie stopped playing, looked up, and smiled. "Olivia!" she said. Dovie wore a dress with a collar that looked like a crocheted doily. Trixie saw doilies everywhere, on the end tables, on the arms and backs of chairs.

"She the runt of the litter?" asked Effie Blackburn, when Dovie introduced them to everybody. Effie, unlike her sister, looked like a man. She sat spreading like a blob of melting butter across the settee, rummaging through her pocketbook. Ollie Pearl had told Trixie in advance that Effie was not all there and could be a little mean. "How come they didn't send her to the orphan home?" Effie said.

"Now, you hush, Effie," Dovie said. "She's not from any litter. She's an *only child*."

"How do?" Old Jack said out of one side of his mouth. A half-chewed stub of a cigar hung out the other. The retired Southern Railroad engineer Ollie Pearl had spoken of, he looked like Humpty Dumpty in pin-striped overalls. He tipped his duckbill cap and went right back to the radio, where "Believe It or Not!" had just started.

Edna Templeton, Ollie Pearl's sister-in-law and the one who owned the house, came in to greet them, hands on her aproned hips. She looked like Abe Lincoln's evil twin sister. Trixie looked down.

"Is the girl that backward, or is she just enthralled with the knots in my pine floor?"

"She's just nervous around new people, Edna," Ollie Pearl said.

Edna's fifteen-year-old son, Frank Junior, leaned in the doorway between the foyer and the parlor. "Shoot!" he said. "We oughta be scared of *her*!" He grinned, his face all teeth. "Somebody put a sack over her head! Hurry!"

Naomi, tall, slim, and dark in a white frock and apron, looked in from the kitchen and stabbed Frank with her eyes.

The Colonel walked over from where he had stood by the fire, quietly smoking a cigar. He laid his hand on Trixie's head and smiled down on her. Then he took both of Ollie Pearl's hands. "Olivia," he said, his voice deep and rich as warm fudge.

Trixie spent the first little while of day one exploring the big house, sticking her head between the rails at the stair landings, and standing on her tiptoes to look out the windows at the blue hills that stretched away out of sight. All the rooms on the backside of the house had what Ollie Pearl called French doors, tall doors with lots of glass panes. They led out onto a big terrace that had steps down to the rocky backyard.

From the terrace, Trixie could see what looked like a small orchard, the rooftop of a house up a slope beyond the inn, the shot of steam from a locomotive tugging up the grade. She could see the rooftops of town and the depot with its steep, fanciful roof.

Beyond the terrace, the yard stretched toward some woods. To the right of a tall spruce tree and a woodshed grew a dark wedge of twisty laurels with what looked like a path running through it. The kitchen, situated downstairs and at the back of the house, looked out on this view, too.

The house had lots of empty rooms, some open or with doors ajar, some locked, others unlocked. Trixie went from door to door, rattling the knobs, peeping through the big keyholes, nosing through the open rooms.

The Blackburn sisters had a phonograph in their room. "Happy Days Are Here Again" by Benny Meroff and His Orchestra lay on top of a stack of records. She danced around singing, "Happy days are here again! The skies above are clear again!" She robbed an umbrella from one corner and pranced around the room, sword fighting with an imaginary opponent. "It's all in the blade, knave!" she declared, taking a swipe at Effie's big bloomers hanging from a line strung over the radiator.

In one room with the door open she saw bony, limp-haired Hissy ironing a bed sheet. Hissy looked like she had crawled out of a potato sack. "Hey!" she said to Hissy, who looked up at her and scowled. Trixie shrugged, walked past the laundry room door, then turned and poked her head back in, sticking out her tongue at Hissy.

Before supper she watched Naomi hoist the beef roast out of the Dutch oven and onto a big platter. Naomi let her stand up on a stool and scoop up the potatoes and onions, which had gone all sticky brown and golden in the pot. Trixie ladled them around the roast.

"Look at her!" Frank said when they sat down to supper. "Her head hardly comes up over the table!"

"Don't pay none of them no mind," Naomi told her when Trixie helped her in the kitchen after supper, "'specially Mr. Frank."

Naomi sometimes stayed long after supper on nights near Christmas when she was doing all her baking. She tied a big apron around Trixie's little waist and told her she was going to help bake mice. "Here, close your eyes and stick out your tongue. This one just came out of the oven." She laid something on Trixie's tongue, something tasting of vanilla and confectioner's sugar that melted clean away.

Trixie opened her eyes again, and Naomi showed her a whole baking sheet full of the thimble-sized mounds of shortbread dough she called white mice. Naomi baked them, and Trixie, standing on the stool at the big metal pastry table, rolled the ones warm out of the oven in a little pile of powdered sugar.

Another day, while the others gathered around the radio to listen to "Sherlock Holmes on the Air," Naomi showed her how to make ornaments by dipping prickly sweet gum balls in water then in flour to make them look snow-covered. In the woodstove warmth of Naomi's kitchen, with the ever-present leafy green framed in the many panes of the wide windows, the secret storm at last began to calm down.

Going to Town

One day Trixie stood up on her stool drying the dishes Naomi washed. Naomi looked dreamily out the window and said she wished Frank didn't have the old Plymouth torn up where it didn't run. She'd like to send Rafe into town for some almond flavoring for pound cake.

"It's foolish to take the car out for such as that, anyway!" Edna said. She wouldn't stand for anything she took as a slight toward her Frank.

"Yes'm," Naomi said. She agreed that was wasteful.

"Before I got so old," Naomi told Trixie, "I used to walk to town almost every day in good weather." The people who stayed there during the inn's heyday used to do the same, she said. She pointed out the kitchen window to an opening in the woods a few yards to the right of the woodshed and the spruce tree. "Used to go right down that path—was a good bit wider in those days—over the creek to the railroad track. Took a right, followed the track straight into town."

"Besides," Edna went on, "we've got a whole bottle of vanilla, don't we? It's wasteful in these hard times to buy anything we don't absolutely have to have."

"Yes'm, and we got coconut and rum flavor and lemon, too, but Mister Frank 'specially likes my five-flavor pound cake. I had in my mind to make one for my Christmas present to him. It calls for almond flavor, too."

Well, that was all Naomi had to say for Edna to give her the go-ahead. When Trixie said she'd love to walk to town, Edna said, "Take some money from the cookie jar, then, and pick me up a bottle of Syrup of Pepsin. My stomach feels sour. I assume we have plenty of flour, Naomi?"

"Yes'm, just about." She looked into the flour bin. "Cuttin' it kind of close, though, with all the baking lately. And I've not made the stack cake yet."

"Might as well get some more. Take Frank with you, Trixie. He can pull it home in the wagon, by the road."

"Oh! Can't I go by myself?" She had her hand in the cookie jar then.

"No! You can't pull a twenty-pound bag of flour by yourself! He's upstairs. Here, take these clothes up for Hissy to iron, while you're at it." She handed Trixie a pair of Frank's denims and a wrinkled white shirt.

Trixie found her way to the ironing room, but she didn't see Hissy there. A half-ironed shirt lay draped across the board, and steam oozed from the holes in the iron. Hearing voices behind Frank's closed door, she thought she'd take a little peep through the key-hole, and when she did, she saw Frank and Hissy horsing around in bed. She knocked—three hard, fast raps—on the door and watched, snickering, while Frank and Hissy, so skinny she looked wormy, hustled to unscramble from the twisted sheets. They sure put on some more show! She ran to her room, laughing so hard she snorted, put on her coat, and stashed the money in her coat pocket. She sneaked down the back terrace and cut through the woods at the side of the house, hoping Naomi or Edna wouldn't spot her from the kitchen window. She didn't want them to see her going without Frank as Edna had instructed.

It had put her in good spirits, making Frank and Hissy squirm. She danced sprite-like on her way down the path through the twisted laurels until, a few yards in, the path made a turn, and she looked back to see the lighted end of the tunnel disappear. She felt a new, delicious chill and breathed in the damp, rooty smell. Her frosty breath made clouds of fairy dust in the air. She pulled her hood up and over her head. *Ooooh! Dark and cold in Little Red Riding Hood's forest!* Farther in, a shelf of rock hung over the path. She jumped up and tried to touch it. Not long afterward, the ground under her feet dropped off, and she had to use the roots and rocks like stairsteps. Beyond the drop she found a wide stretch of hemlock-shaded creek bank. So quiet, except for the gurgling of the creek! She squatted at creek's edge and watched the cold water sluice over the green moss growing on the rocks. Arms stretched out for balance, she crossed the creek over the slick, wet stones and found the railroad tracks beyond a patch of woods and bramble. She walked then skipped then walked along the railroad ties toward town, counting the ties as she went.

In Saluda, men in railroad uniforms and striped caps like Old Jack's sat on benches in front of a line of wall-to-wall brick stores. She wandered inside Thompson's Store, where she watched the lady at the cash register, whom she heard somebody call Miss Lola, pinning the receipts together with safety pins. Outside Pace's general store, a flop-eared dog lay coiled into a donut against the cold. Two women wearing earmuffs and stoles paraded along the sidewalk, their long coats swinging as they walked. Soon after she arrived, she could hear the train *chuff chuff chuff chuff* up the grade. A short while later, the Carolina Special coughed and came to a halt. Winter was the slowest time of year; only a few passengers trickled off the train, some to the diner and the shops, most to Mr. Pace's store.

She followed them to the store, and that's where she first saw

Esther, hair falling to the nape of her neck in gleaming waves, through the awning-shaded store window. A baby-faced boy leaned on the counter, smiling up at Esther. She giggled at something he said, all the while taking money and giving change to customers who came in off the train wanting cigarettes, newspapers, snacks. Trixie walked into the store and stood in one corner just watching Esther ring up sale after sale on the fancy brass cash register, then pause to cut off a hunk of cheese or serve up a pickled egg out of the big glass jar on the counter. All that time she hung on the boy's words, smiled at the customers, showed them where to find what they needed, without getting the least bit flustered.

Behind the counter, at the back of the store, Mr. Pace showed a customer a can of engine grease. A ragamuffin boy, cap pressing down on his brownish hair, pushed a broom between the aisles. Trixie found the almond flavoring. She asked Esther for the Syrup of Pepsin, and Esther, smiling, took a big brown bottle from the rack behind the counter. She stuffed it in a bag along with the flavoring and a stick of sassafras candy, and handed it to Trixie, giggling again at something her boyfriend said. Trixie recognized in Esther Dewberry—Dewberry was her maiden name—the patina of sophistication Ollie Pearl had spoken about. Trixie thought maybe some of it could rub off on her, but she'd have to come back when lover boy had pulled himself away. When she left, she noticed the boy at the back of the store sweeping grit into a dustpan.

She knocked around town a bit and looked in the shop windows until the steam whistle blew and the train *chug-chug, chug-chugged* on its way. Carrying her small parcel, she walked along the tracks far behind the train and came again to the creek, but the terrain looked different there. Across the creek towered a steep hill studded with big boulders of granite. She'd found herself upstream from where she had started.

She knew she had to cross back over the creek and go downstream to find the path, but something upstream caught her eye: A little way to her right, the sun pierced through the huge and witchy branches of an old oak, and not far from it sat an old abandoned boxcar.

She ran up to it and took her time nosing around. She jumped up to see inside the car, but she was too short to see anything but a lantern dangling from a back corner of the ceiling. Somebody had strung a length of rope between two small trees and had draped two dingy, ragged bath towels across it. They each had "LT" monogrammed on them, just like the towels at Laurel Terrace. A lump of soap tied to a string hung from the tree, too. She found a round mirror dangling from a nail on the trunk of the big oak. Near the circle of charred nuggets where somebody had lately made a campfire, she found a couple of tin tubs and several sizes of tin cans, a beat-up aluminum coffeepot and some cups, a tin plate, and a bent spoon.

On a tree stump near the fire pit, she found a pile of wood shavings, a little carving tool, and an oval of wood a little bigger than her palm. She picked up the wood and ran her finger over what looked like the beginnings of a nose, a mouth, and a long beard. "You need some eyes," she said to it. She sat down on the edge of the stump and picked up the tool. She had started to press the sharp tip of it into the wood, in a spot above and to the right of the nose, when a gust of wind stirred in the branches of the big tree and, playfully it seemed to her, showered her with dead leaves that had hung on through the autumn. She looked up into the ragged weave of tree limbs and shadows. Feeling both teased and chastened, by whom she couldn't guess, she placed the wood and the tool back exactly as she had found them.

She walked upstream a few yards to where she could just make out the peaked tops of tents and the flat roofs of tar-paper shacks—a hobo jungle like the one she'd seen on the train ride up the mountain. She saw smoke curling up from a campfire and a scarecrow man sitting hunched over beside it, staring into the fire. She didn't care to go farther. The creek rushed harder here; she had to take every step across the stones with care. She followed the creek back downstream and soon found the path through the laurel. She looked back before she started home, though. She couldn't think why, but she had a pretty good idea she'd see that place again.

The Vagrant

"I thought I told you to take Frank with you!" Edna said soon after Trixie got home, without the twenty-pound bag of flour and without Frank.

He half hid behind the door of the icebox, opening a bottle of milk.

"I asked him," Edna said, "and he told me it was the first he heard of it."

Trixie stared down Frank with blackmail eyes. "Ask him again."

He looked away and kept chugging down the milk.

Edna looked at him. "Frank?"

"Okay. She asked me, and I said I had better things to do."

"Ha!" Trixie broke out into giggles, thinking of Frank and Hissy and their nervous, naked dance. She grabbed her sides. She snorted.

"What's the matter with you?" Edna said, swatting at Trixie's bottom. "I ought to tie you up!" She reached into the broom closet, took out the feather duster, and handed it to Trixie. "Go upstairs and dust everything. And I mean *everything*."

Trixie dutifully dusted the room she shared with Ollie Pearl, as well as the Colonel's room, where she found a tin of mustache wax she just had to open and stick her finger into. From his fancy cigar box she plucked a cigar, stuck it in her mouth, and, putting on an air of refinement, drew it from her lips. "Olivia," she said in a deep, smooth voice.

In Old Jack's room she found a small model of a red caboose and an ashtray full of cigar stubs. She walked right past Frank's room; he could choke in dust for all she cared!

She picked through the records in the Blackburn sisters' room. Fred Astaire's "Puttin' on the Ritz" lay on top this time, and after it, Guy Lombardo's "You're Driving Me Crazy!" One record album caught her eye. It had "Aloha!" on the cover and a picture of an almond-eyed man in flowered boxer shorts and a flowery lei. She put the disk on the sisters' phonograph and listened to the whiney steel guitar above the *bump, scratch, bump, scratch, bump, scratch* of the needle against the grooves.

She yanked Effie's bloomers off the clothesline above the radiator and stepped into one leg and wrapped the bloomers around her—almost three times! She plucked a flowery sprig from a vase of plastic pink and blue flowers and stuck it in her hair. She was standing in front of the mirror, swirling her hips like a hula dancer, when Effie waddled into the room, threw her arms up, and hollered.

Trixie screamed and dodged Effie to get out of the room and into the hall. Effie lumbered down the hall after Trixie, swatting at her. Effie stood at the top of the stairs, bellowing like a stuck hog, as Trixie, still wrapped in the bloomers, lurched to the bottom of the stairs, where Edna, Frank, Old Jack, Dovie, Ollie Pearl, and the Colonel huddled with alarmed faces.

"What in tarnation?" Old Jack said.

"I don't know what you're going to do about her, Ollie Pearl!" Edna hollered. "Watch this!" She held up her hands for all to see, then ran her palms rough and hard down the sides of her apron. "I wipe my hands of her!"

That evening and the whole of the next day, Edna and Ollie Pearl made Trixie stay in her room, but the following night, the snowy night she would always remember, they lightened her sentence by confining her to the kitchen under Naomi's watchful eye. They thought of it as punishment, and she took care to pout about it a little so they wouldn't guess how much she loved it.

Naomi had made the fruitcake a while back—"so the flavors could marry," she said—but that night she took it out of the pie safe and unwrapped it. She gave Trixie the job of covering it with apple jelly to make it shiny. Then Naomi showed her how to ring the top of the cake with slices of pineapple and put a cherry in the middle of each circle. Naomi had taken a pan of gingersnaps, rolled paper thin, out of the oven and set them out to cool.

"You're a cruel woman, Naomi," the Colonel said from the parlor, where everybody sat by the radio waiting for Jack Benny to come on. "The smells wafting in here could drive a man to delirium."

Ollie Pearl tapped his hand and tittered like a bird.

Under her breath Naomi said, "Wonder how anybody can smell anything in there with all that cigar smoke."

A few minutes later Trixie took a platter of gingersnaps to the parlor for everybody to sample. Frank lay on the floor leafing through a comic book. Edna knitted, and Dovie smoked a cigarette and flipped through a magazine, while Effie sat with her hands on her pocketbook, scowling at Trixie. Ollie Pearl worked halfheartedly at crossstitching a sampler, while, beside her, the Colonel smoked his cigar with a regal air. Old Jack used one side of his mouth to chew a stub.

"Jell-O, folks!" Jack Benny said, the way he always started his program, with a commercial.

Old Jack sat like a toad on an ottoman by the radio and twisted the knob to try to clear the static.

Dovie took a warm cookie from the plate. "Naomi!" she yelled toward the kitchen. "You're going to have us all so fat, we can't walk!"

Naomi laughed. "Mis'ry loves comp'ny!"

The Colonel took a nibble and said, "It certainly has a sharp edge to it."

"A gingersnap ain't a gingersnap if it don't bite back!" Naomi said.

When Trixie returned to the kitchen, she saw Naomi standing over the long sink, washing up a bowl, grinning out the window. "What're you smiling at, Naomi?"

Naomi's eyes slid Trixie's way, then back down to the sink. "Li'l bit of snow comin' down," she said and walked over to stoke up the fire in the stove.

Trixie jumped up, held herself over the sink, and looked out. Sure enough, she saw a fine, misty snow falling. She also saw a pair of eyes hanging right outside the window in the dark above the trash can. Slowly, a face filled in around the eyes. Then a mop of brown hair, covered up by a cap. Then a heavy wool sweater. Teasing eyes, frisky grin, fuzzy chin. The boy she'd seen sweeping in Pace's Store? She couldn't tell for sure. She spread her eyes wide. "Naomi!"

That startled the boy, who dropped the lid, clattering, against the can, which made a racket that caused Red and Blue to bark, then another dog somewhere. Naomi frowned and waved the boy on, and he scrambled away into the woods.

By then all the dogs from three counties had chimed in, which started Edna barking. "What's that? Naomi! Has that tramp come around again?"

"No, ma'am! Ain't no tramp. Just an ole coon in the garbage can."

"Well, what's he after?"

Naomi hooted. "Seein' he's in the garbage can, reckon he's after garbage," she mumbled.

"We'd better not be throwing away food in this house!"

Frank jumped up off the floor, reached in a hall closet, and put on his jacket. He grabbed his rifle. "I bet it was too that bum! I'm goin' to chase him down and make him dance!"

"Stop where you are, boy," the Colonel said. "Only a fool takes up arms without a cause."

"I just aim to give him a good scare is all. Maybe just a grazing."

"No, Frank, no!" Edna cried out. "He might have a gun, too!"

"Ain't never been no hobo what carried a gun," Old Jack said out of the side of his mouth where the cigar didn't hang.

Naomi ran in from the kitchen, briskly wiping her sudsy hands with her apron. "You shoot that boy, I shoot you!"

"Mind your place in this house, Naomi!" Edna said, grabbing Frank by the arm. "Please, son."

He jerked away, flew out the door, and disappeared in the woods.

Two minutes later, Frank yelled out "Hey!" They heard a shot. Edna wailed. Then another shot. A long moment passed with Edna whimpering and Effie bellowing before Frank stormed into the house, grinning big-toothed, holding up a sack of something. He held it high like a bird he had bagged.

Naomi stared him down like a bull.

"Hold your horses, Naomi," Frank said. "I just fired in the air to get 'im jumpin', like I said. Him and that ole half-breed hound that trails him everywhere."

"You better be sure about that."

"I am, I am. Next time'll be another story, though. I know where to find 'im, too. He's took over that old boxcar down by the tracks, down at the creek where the other bums camp out.

"Look here what all he got out of our garbage can, Mama."

Edna took the sack, and everybody watched as she pulled out a huge hunk of ham wrapped in a biscuit. She pulled out a baked sweet potato, wrapped in foil and still so hot she dropped it. It fell with a splat onto the floor. She took out a big wedge of pound cake wrapped in wax paper. She found a tin of white mice.

"Mighty well-dressed garbage," Edna said, eyeing Naomi. "Naomi, I have told you and told you that those tramps are like dogs—feed them and we'll never get rid of them!"

"Now, Edna," the Colonel said, "would it hurt to extend a little Christian charity at this time of the year?"

"Charity, my big toe! Those bums are no better than roaches; give one a nibble, and they all come around. Don't give them a crumb, they'll get on up the road to sucker off somebody else."

"Worryin' over nothin'," Old Jack said. He sang out his words like W. C. Fields. "Just that hobo boy, name of Hobo Joe. Bo Joe, other 'boes call him. Ain't more'n fifteen year old. Boy wouldn't swat a fly to save his soul."

"Now how can you know that?" Edna snapped.

"Seen him in town sweepin' up at the store. Me and him talked railroad."

"Just because he can sweep and 'talk railroad' hardly makes him respectable!"

"I'd have to agree with you, Edna," Ollie Pearl said.

"The ladies do have a point there, Jack," the Colonel said.

Old Jack shook his head. "I'll allow you've got good and bad in every profession—"

"Profession!" Edna rolled her eyes.

"But most of your hoboes," Old Jack continued, "they've got a code of honor. I once knowed a hobo who killed another one what stole a silver teapot from an old woman he'd chopped hardwood for."

"Oh, well! Now, that's reassuring!" Edna said.

Old Jack laid a hand on his pained hip and declared himself

ready for bed. "Boy's been here two, three weeks, just about done what payin' work there's to do hereabouts, more'n likely be gettin' on down the road before the week's out—'specially considering what a dandy 'Merry Christmas!' he got here."

That night in their room, Trixie pressed her nose against a glass pane of the French door and thought of the boxcar, of the campsite, of the half-formed wood carving of a face that she had held in her hand. Then later, while she twisted Ollie Pearl's hair into tight flat pin curls, Ollie Pearl locked eyes with her in the vanity mirror. "I'm not so sure it wasn't a mistake to bring you here, Trixie, what with tramps about the place. I'd feel a lot better about things if you played inside and close to the house while we're here."

"But Old Jack just said good things about Hobo Joe."

"Well, Old Jack doesn't have a young girl to raise!"

A pin curl uncoiled, and Trixie twisted it back.

"And you need to understand that even if that tramp who came around tonight were Saint Peter himself, it certainly would not *look* good for you to be seen anywhere near the likes of him. Your reputation could get ruined for life! Do you understand?"

Trixie nodded.

"I'll trust you, then. I believe Frank will keep that boy away from here, and I'll trust you not to go anywhere near that hobo jungle." Ollie Pearl reached over her shoulder and took Trixie's hand. "I can trust you, can't I?"

"Yes, ma'am," Trixie, said, meaning it the minute she said it. But the next minute, remembering the teasing eyes and frisky grin, she thought, *We'll see, we'll see.*

Sneaking Out

The snow that had started that night kept falling the next day, and by the time dinner was over, snow lay over the backyard soft and smooth as a baby blanket. Trixie stood on her stool by the pastry table in the kitchen, cutting out strips from the pages of the Sears-Roebuck catalog. She made a paste of flour and water and spread it on the ends of each strip. Then she linked the circles one around the other to make a chain to hang on the Christmas tree. Once Trixie had made the paper chain, Naomi taught her how to make stars from the foil lining of the cigarette packages Dovie Blackburn saved for her. Trixie punched a hole in the top with a needle, then ran a piece of thread though each one, making silvery ornaments.

From where she stood, she could see out the kitchen window to the snow-laden branches of the big spruce. The opening to the path that wound through the laurel looked luminous and more inviting than ever in the dark, and she wondered what magic the snowfall had made of the old boxcar and Hobo Joe's camp by the creek.

Once Naomi and Rafe had gone home, and everyone else had been tucked into bed for a while, Trixie put on her hooded coat, a scarf, mittens, and boots. Careful not to wake Ollie Pearl, she slipped out the bedroom door, walked quietly across the terrace and down the steps to the yard, trying not to agitate Red and Blue. She walked down the path, deeper into the dreamy nighttime snowfall, into the deep-cushioned quiet. She sensed even then, young as she was, that she must hang those snowy scenes on the walls in her memory so she could travel back to that time and place from the future, that place where she felt cocooned in a sacred, subdued splendor that was on the earth but not of it.

The snow, which had filtered through the gnarly branches and lay in sifted piles like powdered sugar, lit her way. It drooped from the shelf of the flat rock overhanging the path. She walked under and beyond it, and holding on tight to some branches, she scrambled down the stairs made of roots and rocks. She walked across the field of snow under the hemlocks to where the dark creek trickled between and around the white-capped stones. Upstream, across the creek and through the trees buffering the creek bed from the railroad tracks, an ember of yellow-orange light glowed. It disappeared behind a whipping sheet of snow, then it flickered into view again. She walked alongside the creek in the direction of the light, and a while later she could see the flame dancing inside the lantern in the upper left corner of the boxcar. In the nest of light below it, she could see the cap crowning the top of Bo Joe's head. She spotted a rock she could climb up for a better view. But as she scrambled across some brush to reach it, the crackling of the undergrowth beneath her feet didn't get past a dog's ears.

"Woof! Woof woof!"

Bo Joe jumped up. He leaned out of the door of the boxcar. "Who is it? What d' you want?" His voice said he meant business. "I said, Who is it?!"

"It's . . . it's me!"

"Who the heck fire is 'me'?"

She didn't answer.

"Sounds like a little ole field rat, huh, Boy?"

"Woof! Woof woof!"

"Looky here, you little rat, you done got my dog here shakin' in his shoes!"

"I'm sorry! I didn't mean to!"

"Don't know as I believe that. You armed and dangerous?"

"No!"

"How do I know you're not? You better come closer and let me get a look at you." He jumped down from the boxcar. He and the dog headed toward their side of the creek bank.

Trixie grabbed hold of a tree branch and stepped on the first big flat stone she found. Those stones lay farther apart than the ones she'd crossed downstream, and with the snow, they were slicker. She had to leapfrog from the first one to the next. Near the middle, the creek gushed instead of trickled, and she could make it across only by stepping onto a slick sheet of rock just under the water. She stepped out—

"Wait, you little squirt! Don't go crossing those slick rocks!"

His warning came a second too late. She landed, then slipped on the green slime. The icy water rushed over her, roared in her ears, filled up her nostrils, her mouth, filled her whole body with cold, liquid stone. She went rigid. She felt herself sliding and sliding down a stretch of slippery silt. She felt herself scooped up out of the water, pulled up with quick, firm arms, thrown across his lap, her back slapped again and again as she choked out the water.

He pressed her against the wood-smoky wool of his sweater, wrapped her limp arms around his neck, and held her tight to his chest. He walked fast against the wind down the creek bank, up the path. Had the path ever seemed so long? He took big strides across the backyard of the inn, taking forever—so it seemed to Trixie—to reach the door. The cold stiffened her ears, her eyelids, her lips. She could feel the vibration of his chest as he called out "Hey!" and pounded on the door. "We're okay, now," he said to her. "We're okay."

He pounded his fist against the door again, then again, then again. The dogs barked. Lights flicked on upstairs then down. Voices inside, a shuffling of bodies. The door swung open.

"What is it?" Who are you?"

"Oh! Trixie!"

"What's she done now?"

"Little girl fell in the creek," Bo Joe said.

"And you just happened to be right there at the time?"

"Frank, stoke up the stove! We'll ask questions later. And hurry!"

"I'm hurryin'! I'm hurryin'!"

"Dovie, will you run upstairs and get some dry clothes?"

"Frank, run over and get Naomi!"

"Can't do but one thing at a time, Mama! Can't get the car out, anyhow. Snow's too deep to run it."

"Go!"

"I'm goin'! Can't stand the sight of blood."

"Look, she's scraped up her face and hands!"

Ollie Pearl worked a kitchen towel around Trixie's wet head. Trixie shivered and her teeth clattered.

"Oh! She'll get frostbite! She'll die of pneumonia! Let's get these wet clothes off her this minute!"

Bo Joe took off his hat and nodded to everybody. "I'll go on and get out of the way now so you can do what you have to do. Hope the little girl'll be all right."

"Give the boy something for his trouble," the Colonel said.

Edna stepped toward the stove, where an iron skillet held corn bread Naomi had made earlier. She turned it upside down, shook the hard, round disk out, and shoved it into his hands. "Here," she said.

"I'm obliged to you, ma'am."

"Give him something more than corn bread, Edna," Old Jack said. "Some side meat or something that'll stick to his ribs."

"Wouldn't think of taking any more pay for doing what anybody would do," Bo Joe said as he backed out the door.

"Expect you'll be movin' on up the road soon, Bo Joe?" Old Jack asked.

"Reckon so, sir," Bo Joe said. "More likely sooner than later." He tipped his hat and backed out the door, and for all Trixie knew, he was gone for good.

Hobo Joe

They kept Trixie wrapped in quilts by the woodstove that night and in her own bed for the next day. She had a nasty scrape on her face and bruises all over, but she didn't get frostbite and she didn't die of pneumonia. For a day or so she spoke and ate little, though, letting them believe Death might soon knock on her door. Maybe then they wouldn't punish her or torment her with many questions. Maybe then they wouldn't challenge her simple explanation that she had just been playing in the creek, had slipped, and by miraculous coincidence, Bo Joe had witnessed it.

Ollie Pearl rubbed pneumonia salve on her chest and made her take cod liver oil. Naomi had Rafe trudge through the snowy woods to Madame Phoebia Sullivan's for a jar of her healing potion. She put it by Trixie's bed and ordered her to sip on it all through the day. Edna told Ollie Pearl that Trixie could have the run of the county for all she cared and get into as much trouble as she had a mind to; she hadn't ever had to raise a girl and she was mighty glad of it.

From that point on, different rules applied. Trixie had to stay in the yard, with one exception: she could go next door. Ollie Pearl had heard Edna say that Mrs. Wilcox had a boarder with a girl about Trixie's age. Trixie had already headed out the door when Ollie Pearl said, "Don't go any farther than the Wilcoxes'. And don't stay out too long, or we'll have Frank come looking for you."

When Trixie stepped outside, she could see that the freezing rain and sleet that had fallen in the night now encased the snowy branches. Needles of sunlight shot off the trees all around and on the high peaks. She turned around and around, feeling like a tiny speck at the bottom of a giant crystal. She shook a limb of the spruce tree just to watch the ice crackle and release sprays of snow. She could see the roof of the Wilcox house on a rise beyond the orchard, and she wandered in that direction. Then she climbed on a big flat rock where she could see not just one, but two girls sledding down the slope beside the house. One of them looked up her way and pointed. The other looked up at her and shrugged. Trixie waved but the girls turned away.

Trixie shrugged too. She climbed down the rock and walked across the yard into the dark green tunnel where, on that cold but sunny day, little shards of emerald light broke through the branches. She ran, bouncing along the spongy earth to where the path opened up to the light, to where the shining creek ran between smooth, round, snow-covered stones. Then she made her way upstream to where Bo Joe sat on the other side of the creek, on a fallen log, his back to her.

He sat by the fire with the flop-eared dog lying like a bunched-up blanket by his side. Both Bo Joe and the dog breathed out puffs of fog. Woodsmoke swirled around them, and Bo Joe held his shoulders hunched together in the cold. He held something down on a flat rock, chopping at it.

The dog heard the crackle of brush underneath Trixie's feet and woofed the way he'd done before, his voice hoarse in the frosty air. Bo Joe stopped chopping and turned around. He held his hand over his eyes and squinted against the sun. A big grin spread wide and easy across his face. He tipped his hat. "Well, if it ain't the little rat! Come on over."

She hesitated, fingering the snow-crusted winter berries of some kind of bush next to her.

He pointed upstream. "There's a footbridge right up there."

Sure enough, just a few yards upstream, she saw three sturdy boards she hadn't noticed before.

"Too bad you missed it the other night, huh?"

She crossed the bridge, but the dog woofed and she stayed back.

Bo Joe grabbed the dog by the scruff of the neck. "Come on! This old hound wanted to take a bite out of you, he would've done it the other night," he said, as Trixie walked nearer. "Don't have but two teeth in his whole head, anyhow."

"How do you know?" she asked.

"Just pull up his lips and count 'em!"

She grinned and shook her head.

The dog woofed again and whimpered, but Bo Joe shushed him, took the bent-up spoon she'd noticed the other day, and tossed a few dollops of the stuff from the tin tub onto the snow. The dog jumped right on it and wolfed it down. Bo Joe walked over to another tin tub and turned it upside down for her to sit on. "Here," he said, folding a burlap sack and placing it on the tub, "this way your bottom won't freeze and get stuck to it."

She sat down and held her hands in her lap. Then she watched the little white snowflake pattern on her mittens. Then she watched the toe of her boot kick up the snow. She felt her face turning as red as her coat.

He sat back down on the fallen log. "Good to see the little girl's still livin' after the other night, ain't it, Boy?" he asked the dog. "See you've got some scabs and bruises," he said to Trixie. "I figured you'd be bandaged up all over like a little ole mummy." He had blue eyes, misty, squinty eyes.

"Thanks for helping me," she said to the ground.

"Well, it was my fault, anyhow, calling you over. Pains me to think what could've happened. You would've drowned, sure as the world. Your poor little body would've tumbled across the rocks way down to where the creek's dammed up. Snow would've covered you up. Nobody would've found you till the spring thaw."

He grinned and she did, too. She watched his hands as he scooped up some chopped cabbage and dumped it into the tub. He didn't wear gloves, and the knuckles of his long fingers looked red and raw.

He stirred up the stuff. "You game to try my mulligan stew, little girl? It'll be ready once the cabbage gets boiled down good."

"What is it?"

"You never heard of mulligan stew? Recipe goes like this: Dump some water in a pot, then dump in whatever else you got."

"Anything?"

"Well, except maybe a tomato. I can stomach just about anything you'd give me to eat, except a tomato. Sister, I just about can't take a tomato."

"I don't care much for tomatoes, either."

"Yeah. Me neither. Got slimy little seeds in 'em that look like boogers. But there's days lately I've been hungry enough I'd swallow a whole buzzard raw, with the beak and feathers."

"Yuck!"

He shook his head. "Nah. I'd have to be near about starving; my stomach would have to be suckin' on my backbone to put a buzzard in my mulligan stew. Or a tomato. Or one particular kind of rabbit, but that's another story." He dipped the spoon into the mess again and offered it to her.

She curled up her nose and shook her head.

"Smells like garbage, don't it? It'll taste a far sight better once it simmers a while, anyway." The dog held its nose in the air, twitching. "Well, *he* likes it, don't you, Boy?"

"Why don't you give him some more of it?"

"How come? Try countin' his ribs. Go on."

"I can't! I can't see them."

"That's what I know. That's on account of he's well fed. He can wait a minute, anyhow. Shows him who's boss, too. Dog don't want a friend, wants a pack leader—didn't you know that?"

She shook her head.

"No? I can tell that you ain't ever been inside the mind of a dog. A dog don't think like you or me. Look at him."

She looked at the dog's floppy ears, droopy jaws, wet black snout, and goofy, grinning eyes.

"There's thoughts in that head too deep for words. Going to eat like a couple of kings today, me and him." The dog's tail thumped once, and Bo Joe nodded toward the pan. "Chopped a cord of wood for Mrs. Phoebia Sullivan, and she paid me with a pound of potatoes, a big head of cabbage, and a quart jar of that potion she says cures anything and everything that ails a body. It's been going good here lately, work-wise I mean, though it's drying up, I can tell. Mr. Pace let me sweep out the store the other day, rearrange some cans. Paid me with a couple cans of pork brains in milk gravy."

"I saw you there!"

"Did you for a fact? Didn't see you. Like to keep my nose to the floor when I'm pushin' broom. Like to do a good job, especially for the likes of Mr. Pace. He's a fine man. And Miss Esther's a real fine gal, the one who runs the cash register."

The train whistle sounded from somewhere far away. An old, skinny hobo ambled up from the jungle and squatted by the creek, smoking a cigarette. Bo Joe called out to him: "May I ask if you have plans for dinner, sir? Shall I lay another place at the table?"

The old hobo grinned, showing jack-o'-lantern teeth. "Shall I bring the wine?" he responded in a deep-throated, ragged voice, then went back to his cigarette.

"That there's Scoop Shovel Sam," Bo Joe said. "He don't care for company. I'll take him a tin can full of this here stew when it's good and done." He pointed toward the boxcar. "Tried to get him to jungle up with me, but he likes to stick to himself. He's the only one besides me around right now. Work's dryin' up. Jungle's pretty much dried up, too."

The dog stared at Bo Joe, then the mess cooking on the fire, then at Bo Joe again. The dog thumped his tail. Bo Joe scooped up a big glob of the stuff and dropped it onto the ground. Then another and another. After the dog ate it, he came up to Trixie and nudged her hand. She rubbed her mitten across his muzzle. "Is he your dog?"

"Ask him and he'll say he is. Slung him a bone one day and he latched onto me like a tick, didn't you, Boy?"

"What's his name?"

"Boy. Leastways, when I called him that the first time—'Here, boy!' I hollered—he came at me wagging his tail. Figured that must be his rightful name."

"You ought to give him a real name!"

"Like what?"

"I don't know. Ranger. Or Champ. Or Scout. The coonhounds back at the house, their names are Red and Blue."

"Shoot fire! Dogs that hang out with 'boes, it's cruel to give them names. Dog like that, soon as he takes up with a 'bo, the 'bo goes on down the track and then the dog takes up with the next one. One 'bo calls him Bob, next 'bo calls him Ace. Dog like that goes to town, his head's jerkin' every which way every time a name's called. Can't even go about his business for his head swivelin'."

"Is he a pure-blooded coonhound? Red and Blue are. Red's a red tick and Blue's a blue tick."

"Yep, he's a pureblood. Just like I'm pure Chinese. I won't lie about it. One thing I ain't is a liar. We're just a couple of mutts, me and him both. Just your ordinary Joes, ain't we, Boy? Ain't got no flags to wave. Ran him off one time already. He stayed gone two whole days. Then I woke up one night with him standing over me, them gangly front legs on each side of my head, sliding that slobbery tongue all over my face."

Trixie scratched the dog's chest. "I think he's a nice dog."

"He's all right. Ain't the worst dog ever latched onto me. One time I had a dog I couldn't get shed of, dog who went on to make a name for himself. Remind me to tell you about him."

The dog watched Trixie, all bright-eyed the way a dog will do, like he would surely say something if he could. She clicked her tongue; the dog jumped up and slurped her face. She giggled.

Joe grabbed him by the scruff of the neck and pulled him away. "Back off, Boy! You don't go kissin' the girls on the first date. Yeah, got to be careful letting a dog latch onto you, lovin' him up too good, letting him eat too good."

"I had a dog one time," she said. "He could sit up on his hind legs like this." Trixie lifted her hands to her chest, stuck out her tongue, and panted. "His name was Hot Dog."

"Did you for a fact?" Joe said. "Tell me something, was he one of those long dogs shaped like a weenie, one that walked real low to the ground?"

"Yeah! How did you know?"

"Just had a feelin'."

"Well, anyway, I fed him good, loved him up, like you say, and he was a real good dog."

"Yeah, I hear you, but I still say, do too much of that and a dog starts to talkin'. Spreads the good news around to his buddies. 'I done found me a sucker,' he says to one, then that one passes it around. First thing you know, all the dogs around got wind of it. You hear dogs barking in the night and you think they're barking at the moon or treeing coons; truth is, they're talking between themselves, comparing notes about how to get to where the gettin's good."

"I don't believe it! There's no such thing as a dog that talks!"

"That's because you don't understand their talk. You think they don't know how to talk just because you can't figure out what they're saying. Think about the last time you heard somebody talking in the Swahili language. I bet you thought they didn't know how to talk either. Or like that Sullivan woman over in the woods, mumbling over her potions. No such thing as a talking dog, my foot. Besides, folks say there's no such thing as an elf either."

"There's not!"

He grinned and looked at her. "That's what you look like in that little red coat with that pointed hood. An elf."

"I'm not!" she said, grinning big, trying not to.

"Ain't so sure about that."

"There's no such thing!" she said.

"Ain't so sure about that either. Look here, your shoe's untied." He leaned over to tie it. "I tell you what, little girl. We been talking all this time and we ain't had what I'd call a proper introduction. Other night I heard them up at the house call you Pixie. Shoot, that even sounds like an elf, don't it?"

"Trixie!" she said. "Trixie Hogan."

"Trixie? Well, I'm Joe and I'm a hobo. My official name, I guess you'd call it, is Hobo Joe. Other 'boes call me Bo Joe, sometimes just Bo, but some folks call me just Joe. Got all that?"

"Yeah. Old Jack told us your name."

"Oh yeah? I must've created a big stink up there the other night when I was upending that garbage can. That boy who come shooting at me must've been your boyfriend."

"Oh, no he's not!"

"Well, I'm glad to hear it. He come down here one night, prowling around, game to start some trouble with me. We had us a tussle and I gave him notice. Don't think he'll come back. Are you sure he's not your boyfriend?"

"No!"

"You're not sure?"

"Yes, I mean, no! I mean, I'm sure he's not my boyfriend!"

"I bet he is. I bet you got a bunch of boyfriends."

"I don't!"

"Nah, I reckon you don't. You're not old enough. You're just a little pipsqueak kid. What are you—eight years old, maybe nine?"

"I'll be twelve years old in April!"

"For a fact? Eleven years old." He shook his head.

"Almost twelve!"

"When I was your age," he said, like he was fifty and not fifteen, "I was walking along the tracks down around Waycross, Georgia, where I lived, dreaming about catching out a freight and heading across the whole country. Or else I was down on the Suwannee fishing. I thought *those* days were hard." He shook his head at the thought.

"How come you left?"

"Daddy died, Mama got married again. I was one too many mouths to feed. They shut the school down, no work, nothing to do. One fine morning I wrapped up what I could in my pillowcase, wrote "I'll write" on an envelope, laid it on the kitchen table, and hopped a freight to anywhere. Ended up going anywhere and everywhere, and I mean everywhere. Hadn't gone twenty-five miles down the track, though, till I figured out riding the rails wasn't no easy life. I wanted to go home but couldn't do it."

"How come?"

"Wasn't anything to go back to. Set my mind on going down the tracks, root hog or die."

"What did you do? I mean for money, for food?"

"Well, the first thing I did was hop off the train and find a circus set up outside a town. Got me a job there, cleaning up after the animals. Did that whenever I could. Learned a powerful lesson working carnivals and circuses."

"Like what?"

"Found out that no matter how hard times get, no matter where you go in the world, there's always some dookie for you to shovel."

Trixie giggled.

"Stumbled into a job helping out a carpenter one time. Then I cut timber in Washington state, hoed corn in Iowa, drove steel in Michigan." He held up his arm and made a fist. "That's where I got this muscle. Got one in my other arm just like it. Go on, sock it. Go on. I won't even feel it." He shut his eyes tight.

She hit it hard, and her small fist bounced right back off. She did it again, harder. And then again. Then she laid into it with two fists.

He didn't even flinch! A few seconds later, he yawned and opened his eyes. "Go on and sock it!" he said. "I been waiting."

"I did already!"

"You did? Shoot fire, I sure couldn't tell it."

A Dog's Life

Joe tried to convince her that when he was a little kid like Trixie, he had all kinds of special talents. "I used to know how to breathe through one lung at a time," he said. "I swear!"

She was squealing with laughter when she heard Frank calling her. "Bye!" she told Bo Joe. "I gotta go!" She turned and scrambled like a monkey across the footbridge over the creek.

Frank met her at the head of the path. "Get home, you little piss ant! Where've you been? You been hanging down there with that bum, like some trashy little kid whore?"

"You want me to tell your mama how I peeped through the keyhole and watched you and Hissy doing something ugly?" She kicked him in the shins.

"Ow! You little shit!"

"I'll do it, too!"

"Well, now!" Ollie Pearl said when Trixie came in. She sat by the fire with the Colonel, looking at the photo album Edna kept with pictures made during the inn's heyday.

Naomi helped Trixie out of her coat. She put her hand on Trixie's cold cheek and shivered. "You look like you had a big time!"

"Was she a nice little girl?" Ollie Pearl asked. "The one whose family is boarding at Mrs. Wilcox's?"

"Yeah, she's real nice," Trixie said. *Well, she probably was, once you got to know her.*

During the few but full days that followed, Trixie was grateful for the Colonel. He and Ollie Pearl looked across the table at each other, moon-eyed. They sat in the parlor, exchanging life histories. When Frank got the old Plymouth going again, they took it to see Ralph Justice, an ailing cousin of Ollie Pearl's, in Hendersonville. Otherwise, Ollie Pearl would have focused her attention on Trixie and would have tuned in to her delinquency.

Frank left her alone, either because he had taken her intent toward blackmail to heart or because he figured she wasn't worth messing with. He spent most hours of most days helping Rafe chop wood, or taking apart a couple of junk cars he kept under a shed behind the garage, or running the roads with some hoodlums he'd taken up with down in Melrose.

Edna had wiped her hands of her.

Naomi—kind, knowing Naomi—never let her leave the house for those supposed playdates with the girl boarding at the Wilcox place without a small sack of whatever they'd had leftover from dinner.

"Where's Boy?" Trixie asked the next time she visited Bo Joe.

"Off hunting squirrel, if he knows what's good for him. Told him I had a hankering for some squirrel meat for supper."

Everything in Hobo Joe's camp fascinated Trixie, as did all she began to learn about the way the hoboes shared things. A 'bo who'd camped there earlier had hung a little, round mirror from a nail on the tree next to the boxcar. He'd left it there so the 'boes who came after could look in it to shave. Joe didn't look like he cared much for shaving. Another 'bo had also left the frypan and a bent spoon and a tin pie plate that he used, as well as the lantern hanging from the ceiling inside the boxcar.

"Now, a tramp or a bum would take all this stuff and hock it in the next town," Bo Joe said, "but a genuine 'bo would shoot hisself in the foot first.

"I'll show you something else." He picked Trixie up by the waist and sat her in the door of the open boxcar. She looked down and imagined sitting there speeding along the tracks in the dark night in the open air. "This here is the liberry," he said, pulling a cardboard box from the corner next to a pile of burlap sacks. Every 'bo that comes around, if he takes a book, is supposed to leave one. My good buddy, Jungle Buzzard, his mama lives down around Green River. He brings a little stash every time he stops by."

They sat in the open door of the boxcar, their feet swinging, while Joe lugged onto his lap a huge book called *Anthony Adverse*. Trixie told him it looked like an awfully long book, but Joe swore he'd read the whole thing. The library also had lots of *National Geographic* magazines with pictures of blue oceans and high mountains and half-naked people with pierced ears. He showed her a beat-up copy of *Tarzan, Lord of the Jungle.* He'd read it three times, he said.

He yanked a tight roll of blankets onto his lap, and she asked, "What's that?"

"My bindle. What I carry with me and unroll to sleep on. I keep all my worldly possessions in it, too."

"All of them?"

He nodded. "Ever heard the saying 'You can't take it with you'?"

Trixie said she had.

"Well, when I die—us hoboes call it 'going westbound'—all the 'it' I can't take with me will fit right in here." He slapped the bindle as he would the back of an old friend.

The dog didn't stay gone long. "What d'you bring me, Boy?" Joe called out.

Boy thumped his tail, then shuffled toward them, tail between his legs.

"See that look on his face? Like he's been to town and Miss Esther slipped him a stick of beef jerky. I do believe I've done hooked myself up with a town dog. Town dog gets handfed, can't hunt, can't even retrieve a stick. Ain't got one ounce of ambition."

"You're being mean to him!"

"Oh, I ain't."

He whistled and the dog jumped up into the boxcar and licked both their faces. Trixie scratched the dog behind the ears.

"It's a bad thing for a 'bo to get attached to a dog," he said. "You can't ride the rails with a dog. When you head off, you have to leave 'im behind and he has to find somebody new. It's a regular heartbreaker." He looked at Boy and said, "Don't know if I'll regret getting shed of you or not."

"Oh! You're going to hurt his feelings!"

"Nah. He ain't the peskiest dog I've ever had trailing me, though, I'll give him that. Had a dog one time who followed me from town to town. Followed me everywhere I went, sometimes beat me to town. I swear I don't know how he did it. Kind of spooked me, that dog did."

"What do you mean?"

"Well, I gave him his walking papers when I caught out a freight in Birmingham. One week later, I walked into town outside of Fort Worth, and there stood that same dog—I'm telling you the truth— one leg cocked up, peeing on a lamp post. 'What the heck took you so long?' he asked me.

"Before him, I had a purebred coonhound hanging at my heels. An English coonhound. That particular dog took up with me while I was hoeing corn in Iowa. The man I worked for, it was one of his hunting dogs, and the dog walked up to where I was camped by the tracks. We got to talking, me and that dog, nothing to amount to much, just your ordinary chewing the fat by the fire, you know. Then he told me he was a breed of dog called an English coonhound and his name was Chauncey. But you sure couldn't tell it from the way he talked."

Trixie giggled. "How come?"

"'Cause that breed of dog, an English coonhound, wouldn't you expect him to talk like the king or queen of England or somebody? Dogs from Iowa talk real country, though. That's the kind of thing you learn on the road. Like I said, he took to trailing me, and before long we started having what you might call too much togetherness. He talked too much; he was bad to brag. We'd play checkers with some old men in front of the store, and he'd beat me every time. I'd start telling a tale and he'd butt in with the punch line. And he right fast unlearned how to hunt. Before long I was hoeing corn and pushing broom to keep me and him both up. One day I said to him, 'You get on now. I can't take no more of you shaming me. And I can't scrounge up enough grub to feed myself, much less me and you both.'

"He looked pitiful, I tell you what, his ears hung plumb to the ground. He said to me, 'But I ain't got nowheres else to go.' Like I said, he was a real country talking dog. I said to him, 'Well if you're planning on running with me for a while, you'll have to quit showing me up and shaming me. And you figure out a way to earn your keep, or you're hittin' the road.'

"Day or two later, I got wind of some work at a big fancy house with uppity people living it, folks who'd held on to their money somehow or other. I knocked on the door and the woman said, 'You can clean out my gutters and weed my garden, but I won't have stray dogs around here.' About that time the dog spoke up and told her his name was Chauncey and he begged her pardon, he was not a stray, but a purebred English coonhound. He cut loose and told this long tale about how he'd lived all over the world and had worked as a butler in London, England, for the Baring family, who owned the Baring Bank of England. He said they would be pleased to give her references. Did she happen to have need of a butler?

"The woman looked down at Chauncey and cocked her head to one side. You could tell by the look on her face that something about the situation didn't add up in her mind. She was looking pretty darn suspicious. Finally, she said to him, real snooty-like, 'Strange that you didn't pick up the accent.'"

Trixie bent over double, snickering. "You're making that up!"

"I am not! Day came she didn't have any more work for me to do, but she kept him on. He moved on up in the world. I gave him a leg up; now he's got more than me. Last I heard tell, that dog was over there in England working at the Parliament. Wears one of them curly white wigs to work five days a week.

"You're looking like you think I'm pulling your leg, but I tell you what, you ride the rails as long as me, nothing would surprise you, especially if you work the circus for a while. I've seen it all: the frog boy, the monkey girl, man who could stand inside a 600-degree oven until a leg of lamb cooked. Then he'd walk out with nary a blister! But the one that sticks in my mind is the long-legged rabbit."

"I saw a long-legged rabbit one time!" Trixie said. "Its back legs were this long!" She held out her hands to show how long.

"Did you, for a fact? Well, what you saw was a hare. They've got four legs with pretty long back legs. What I'm talking about is a two-legged rabbit with legs as long as a man's. Stands up straight like a man, too. Had one last circus I worked at. Now, I knew that long-legged rabbit might be nothing more than a man dressed up as a rabbit. I knew it for sure when I saw him stick a cigarette in his mouth and bum a light off the strong man. Circus and carnival people, they're not straight shooters like you and me. They'll pull the wool right over your eyes. Well, I was never so took away in my life as I was the day I ran into one of those long-legged rabbits, sure as shootin'—in the wild! I took off after it, but it real quick outran me. A rabbit with legs as long as a man's, he's got some more spring to his step. You don't want to eat that breed of rabbit, anyhow. Looks too much like a man." He shook his head. "No, ma'am, I don't want to put something with legs that long in my mulligan stew." He dropped his voice to a whisper and said, "Can you keep a secret?"

"Yeah!"

Joe took a bandanna out of his bindle, unfolded it real slow—made a big deal out of unfolding it—and spread it on the floor between them. She'd never seen chunks of genuine gold before, and she'd seen plenty of nickels but never a wooden one. Joe said he carved the nickel himself. That was a hobo thing. You had to watch out for bums, though. They'd pass off wooden nickels for real, he said. "You ever heard the saying 'Don't take no wooden nickels'?"

"I think so."

"Well, that was some good advice." He had tiger-eye marbles, Civil War coins, and a gold tooth. He showed her a glass eye he said he shook out of a dead man's skull.

"What do you keep that stuff for?"

"Well, it's a good feeling to have a piece of real gold in your pocket. Makes a 'bo feel like he's got something to his name. Get hungry enough, you can buy eats with it, too. And as for the glass eye, when you're riding the rails, you have to be rough and ready. Supposing I was to lose an eye in a fight?" He spit on the eye and polished it with his shirttail. The way he held it up to his own eye, she thought he might try it on. His eye looked big and weird and wavy behind it. "Figure it don't hurt to carry a spare."

She laughed and her hand went straight to her mouth.

He lowered the eye. Then, gently, he pulled her hand away from her face. "What did you do that for? What're you trying to hide that cute smile for?"

"Here's why!" She grinned big and showed him the space between her two front teeth.

"So what?"

She folded her tongue up and stuck it through the gap to show how wide the space was.

He waved it off. "Shoot, you're worried about *that*?"

"Yeah! It's ugly."

"I don't think so. Besides, everything kind of shifts when you grow up, don't you know. In time your bones'll grow, shove those teeth together."

"Really?"

"Sure. You ever known me to tell a lie?"

"How about these?" She pointed to where her bottom teeth sat jumbled like tossed dice.

"Shoot, I bet by the time you're all grown up, they'll be straight as a row of corn."

"You think so, really?"

"Sure they will!" He hopped out of the boxcar and held his arms out. "Jump!" he said. "You better get home. It'll be dark before too long."

"I guess I gotta go?" she said.

"I guess you gotta."

"Will you still be here if I come back?"

He tapped her cheek with his knuckles and said, "I never know when I'll take a notion to hop a freight. If I see my way clear, I might even catch out the midnight freight tonight."

"How come? Why don't you ever just stay in one place? Why don't you stay here?"

"Been here a while already. Got to go where there's a chance I can find work. Gettin' up and goin', that's what a hobo does, don't you know."

"Oh," she said.

He laid his hands on her shoulders. She had to tilt her head back to look up at him, and when she did, the hood fell off her head. He pulled the hood back over her head and tied it a little tighter under her chin.

"But I tell you what," he said. "If—and I mean *if* it happens I'm still here tomorrow—it sure would be a treat to look up and see a little elf come skipping down my way like I did a little while ago."

Spirits of the Forest

That night Trixie dreamed she took long floating strides down the back steps, across the yard, and down the path through the laurel, to find the creek flowing full but soundlessly, the campfire circle cold and snow-covered. Not a footprint or paw print disturbed the inch of fresh snow that had fallen over the whole scene in the night.

When she awoke in the morning, she jumped out of bed and pressed her face to the frosty glass, relieved to find that no new snow had fallen, after all. That much of her dream, at least, had not proved true. She rushed to dress, quietly, so as not to wake Ollie Pearl, but Ollie Pearl awoke and informed her that the Colonel needed to pay a visit to the doctor later in the morning. She insisted they both go with him, in part, Trixie would realize later, because Ollie Pearl wanted her to get used to the idea of the three of them as a family.

Downtown, while they waited in the dim little waiting room for the Colonel to see the doctor, Ollie Pearl could sense her agitation. "What in the world is the matter with you, Trixie?" Ollie Pearl allowed her to take a walk outside, and Trixie felt a flood of relief and a rush of rapture to find Joe outside the depot, pedaling quart jugs of Madame Sullivan's potion.

"Are you afflicted with bursitis?" he yelled to passengers getting off the train, to the porters and the brakemen. "Have you got unexplained hoarseness of the throat? A general malaise or weakness in the limbs?"

He grinned and tipped his hat to Trixie. She smiled and looked down at her shoes.

That afternoon Ollie Pearl and the Colonel stayed so deep in grim-faced conversation, Trixie wondered if he had received bad news from the doctor. She took advantage of Ollie Pearl's preoccupation by walking straight to Joe's camp, where she found him slinging a stick into the creek, trying to make a retriever out of no-talent Boy. Afterward, Joe built another fire, and sometime later they shared a bowl of mush he'd boiled up from the bag of cornmeal Naomi had put into the trash can outside the kitchen for his discovery. She'd hidden a tin of coffee, there, too. The smoky brew took a long time to percolate in the beat-up aluminum pot, but when the brown liquid at last burbled up into the little dome of glass, Trixie had her first taste of coffee. It would never smell as good or taste so hot and rich and strong as it did that day out of those bent tin cups in the cold air by Joe's campfire.

"Reckon I could find a way to sell it by the cup to people getting off the train in town?" he asked. "That's how I sold Mrs. Sullivan's potion today—for ten percent of the proceeds."

"I don't know. Wouldn't most people want to go to the diner, where it's warm, to get their coffee?"

"Yeah. You're probably right. This here tastes a far sight better, though. Can't beat hard creek-water coffee, slow-percolated in burning coals in the raw air." He patted her head and tweaked her chin. "And you sure can't beat the company."

Joe's next idea for making money took them on a long walk in the deep woods, the dog traipsing along behind them, to look for chinquapins. The sweet little wild chestnuts had become rare because of the chestnut blight, so he thought he could sell them outside the train depot for a few pennies a string to travelers and railroad workers. Though he found enough good ones to fill up his coat and britches pockets, most of the nuts he found on the forest floor had ripened a few weeks earlier, so it looked like that plan would fall through.

Trixie and Joe had come to a place where a big sycamore had fallen across a gorge, where far below, the icy water flowed like long white hair between the big boulders. He showed her things she never would have noticed—flakes of lavender moss that grew on big rocks, the different shades of brown in what had looked to her like ordinary brown tree bark. He picked up a gnarled root and turned it around in his hand. "See those eyes?"

"They do look like eyes!"

Neither of them spoke for a while. Somewhere far away a limb snapped under the weight of the snow. The dog's ears perked up.

"Sic 'em!" Joe said. Boy trotted off, made a rustle in some bushes, then the woods went all quiet. Joe stopped and said, "Listen."

"What? I don't hear anything."

"That's just what I mean. Hear how quiet it is? You ever been walking in the woods, nobody's around, but you feel like somebody's there, like somebody or something's watching you?"

Trixie looked around at the upstretched arms of the toffee-hued, snow-coated branches of the trees going on and on as far as she could see. "Like who?"

They walked on. "I don't know exactly," he said, "but sometimes when I've hopped off a freight just shy of a town, I'll take the long way through the woods. Walking along by myself, I guess the quiet kind of plays with my head and I start to think about all the people—animals, too—who are dead now, who've walked in these woods right here, I mean from way, way back. You ever think about that?"

"Ooh! I don't want to."

"Take your pioneers and your Indians and all the people before them, running around nekked with spears, hanging around in caves.

That's a whole heap of dead people. And then you throw in all the animals, from your dinosaurs and your bears and bobcats down to all your little ants and creepy-crawlies, ever since the world started. Even the leaves that fall off the trees. Everything dies, rain falls on it, it rots and turns into that fine silty stuff that slides between your toes when you step into the creek. Then it's all sucked up into everything, into the trees and bushes. You know what I mean?"

"Yeah. . . ."

"Well, some of those somebodies, they're always trying to show theirselves." He held up the gnarled root. "I'll see one in a piece of found wood like this, showing part of a face. I'll work at it and work at it to get the whole face to come up."

As they walked, Joe pointed out features of faces in the woods Trixie hadn't seen before. She picked up a piece of a fallen limb with a knot in it that looked like a bird's eye. The eye within another limb looked for all the world like a snake's. They walked through a grove of huge old trees where the folds and knobby growths looked like whole faces staring out at them, some grinning, some snarling. "This one here's a pouty ole grumble guts," he said about a knot in a tree with the bark twisted into a furrowed brow and a stuck-out lower lip.

A log spanned a narrow place in the creek, and Joe walked on ahead of her so he could turn back and give her a hand to help steady her as she crossed it. Boy came loping up and splashed through the creek behind them. The three of them walked on through the woods, their feet crunching on the frozen leaf mulch that covered the forest floor.

They came to a place where water from the creek fell in long white veils down steep rocks, and Trixie said, "Joe, how'd you know about all these places, no longer than you've been here?"

"Well, kid, when you're riding the rails and you hop off at a place, you know you're a short-timer, and if there's anything worth taking a look at—and there always is—you know you got to take a look at it now."

They walked along the tracks back toward Joe's camp, with Trixie counting the ties under their feet. The dog stepped and stumbled behind them.

"Yeah, it's a hard life, hoboing," Joe said, "but there's always something around the bend, always something new to see around the curve in the track."

Names

Trixie recalled a time at the camp when she watched Joe tear into a fried chicken leg she'd taken from her own dinner plate, slipped into her pocket, and smuggled to him. She stared at him and he caught himself, wiped his mouth with the napkin she had wrapped it in, and said, "Sorry, don't mean to wolf. Way you've been feeding me, ought not to have an appetite. Reckon I'm storing up for the days ahead."

"That's okay," she said, and he lit in again just like he had the first time. It did her heart good. Ollie Pearl had always said it did your heart good to see a man eat.

Afterward, they built a snowman—a snow 'bo, he called it. He said if they built it in the shade, the sun couldn't melt it as fast, so he had chosen a spot in a clump of trees not far from the boxcar. He scooped up the snow with a tin bucket. She couldn't scoop up much snow at a time, so Joe told her to just pat the snow firm once he had it in place. She ran around the snowman, beating the snow hard with her fists until he told her she'd done enough.

She sat down on a tree stump and rubbed the dog behind the ears. "Joe, why didn't you ever tell me your name. I mean besides Hobo Joe."

"Well, didn't see the need. Not too crazy about it, either."

"What is it?"

"Joseph."

"Just Joseph?"

"Joseph Stanley Caldwell."

"I like it!"

"There's worse names, I reckon. Funny thing is, that sounds like somebody else. Whoever you are when you hop a freight kinda melts away with the miles. Before long it's like you really become Hobo Joe. Or Frypan Bill. Or Little Lonesome."

"Are those real people?"

"Yeah. Just some 'boes I know, or know of. I met up with Luther the Jet and Oklahoma Slim at the Chicago World's Fair. Legends in their own time."

"Are there girl hoboes?"

"There's a few. There's Cinder Box Cathy, Minnesota Maggie, and Libby Lump. A lump, that's what we 'boes call food packaged up to take along, like what a waitress at a café might slip you, or what Naomi put for me in the garbage can before you came around. Libby has that name because she's good at going to town and getting lumps. She'll bring them back to the 'boes she's jungling up with. There's a lot of girl hoboes nobody knows who they are. They dress up like boys, don't you know. Have to protect themselves."

"Protect themselves from what?"

"From things," he said. "Things a little girl like you'll have to find out about soon enough."

Little girl!

Joe stepped a little ways into the woods to find enough snow for the head. "I've even met Guitar Whitey," he went on when he came back. "He can tear up a guitar. And Cincinnati Red, reckon he got his name on account of his red hair and he's from Cincinnati. And Slow Motion Joe—moves like dead lice is falling off him, they say. Me, I had a partner one time name of Uncle Hard Times, wandered off from a bunch of harvest tramps when I was picking peaches down around Elberta, Georgia. Looked after him till he fell under the wheels and got what we 'boes call sliced and diced. Been riding by myself ever since. And then there's my good friend everybody calls Jungle Buzzard. He's the one from around here, the one who put me onto this place. I owe him big-time for that."

"If he has a place to live, how come he rides the rails?"

"Some of your 'boes are part time. They take off for a while because they're one less mouth to feed at home. They go looking for work, and if they're lucky to make a few dimes, they bring it back to their folks. They're also game for adventure."

"How'd Jungle Buzzard get a name like that?"

"'Cause that's what somebody started calling him, you know, funnin' him. A real jungle buzzard's a bum who's been at a jungle longer than anybody, calls all the shots, mooches off the other 'boes. J. B., he hangs around a jungle just to teach the newer 'boes the ropes, just to learn them things that'll keep them out of trouble. Talks fancy for a 'bo, though. Can talk the silk right off a worm. And smart! Read the whole encyclopedia he bought for twenty-five cents at the Salvation Army store.

"That hunk of wood, the one I'm trying to get a face to come up out of? I learned if you take your time with it, a piece of wood'll tell you what it wants to be, like I said before. J. B., he's the one who taught me that."

"He must be the smartest man in the whole world."

Joe laughed. "Yeah, except I'd hardly call him a man. Ain't but a couple years older than me."

Trixie's mouth dropped open; she had pictured Jungle Buzzard much older.

"But what I didn't find out about hoboing through hard knocks,

J. B. taught me. He can work the trash cans and dumps better than any hobo I know of. Got some style about it, too. He used to say there wasn't no excuse for a road kid going hungry for long. He said to find a scrap of bread in a garbage can, knock on the door, hold the bread out in your hand. When the woman of the house comes to the door, you tell her you found it in her garbage can, you ask her if you can eat that scrap of bread, and nine times out of ten you'll get you a real good meal out of it.

"Jungle Buzzard, he's the one what got beat with a crowbar by Texas Slim, the mean ole bull in El Paso. Right proud of it, too. Talks it up big."

"He got beat by a *bull*?"

"Shoot, yeah. A railroad bull. They're kinda like police who work for the railroad, keep the hoboes off the trains—or try to. There's a lot of 'em would as soon beat a 'bo's brains out as look at him. Yeah, hoboing, it's hard in ways a little prissy-pants girl like you probably don't even need to know about."

She stamped her foot. "I'm not a prissy pants!"

He raised his eyebrows, surprised at her temper.

"My aunt sent me to finishing school, but the teacher said training me was like teaching a cat to fly!"

He laughed. "What the heck fire kind of school do you go to to get finished?"

"It's this place you go where they teach you good manners and the social graces."

That bowled him over. He buckled over laughing then. "Shoot! Right here in this day and time, in the 1930s? I thought they got all that over with back in eighteen hundred and something. You couldn't hog-tie and carry me to some fool place like that!"

"Me neither!"

"Looks like we have a lot in common, don't it?"

We, he said. *We!*

When they finished with the snow 'bo, Joe took the bucket, hauled water from the creek, and slathered water all over it. The water froze quickly, which gave the snowman a nice sheen. Joe said that would make it harder to melt when the sun hit it, and it would last a lot longer.

She held her chin cupped in her hands and watched him. She thought about his riding the rails, eating out of trash cans, and sleeping in a tar-paper shack or out under the open sky without even a rusty old boxcar for shelter. She noticed holes in his sweater. He needed a companion on his long journey. Somebody who could see to it that he ate more than pork brains and gravy. Somebody who was used to picking up and moving from place to place, who could hang her hat anywhere. Somebody small who wouldn't take up much room in a railcar or get in the way. Her mind spun like a top. By the time he had iced up the snow 'bo, she'd already gone nine hundred miles by his side, cooked up a hundred skillets of mulligan stew, and beat off a hundred railroad bulls with her own personal crowbar.

Bo Joe had found a corncob pipe another 'bo had left in the railcar, and they stuck it in the snowman's mouth. Then he sat down beside Trixie. The snowman looked strange and lovely sitting there just inside the woods in that bare space between some trees, where the skinny shadows of the limbs cut across it at different angles.

"Look at that. Look at what we did, kid."

What we did, he said. *We!*

They shared some roast beef Naomi had sent, and he said, "This sure beats eatin' a piece of bread a dog peed on like I had to one time."

Her nose curled up. "Did you really do that?"

"Sure, I did!"

He took a look at her face and the way she clutched her belly. She thought he'd come loose in the middle, he laughed so hard.

"I tell you what, kid, you wouldn't survive half a day riding the rails!"

"I bet I would too!"

"I don't know." He tweaked her nose. "You're a swell kid and all, but it'd take some more girl to last long as a hobo."

Well, she might just show him sometime. "Joe, how come you keep on calling me 'kid'?"

"'Cause that's what you are. Not even twelve years old yet, just a little ole squirt."

She propped her elbows on her knees and dropped her chin into her hands and pouted.

"What's the matter?"

"I'm tired of being a little squirt. You either get passed over, or else you get picked on, or else stomped on like a bug!"

He laughed and shook his head. "Well, I wouldn't worry too much about it," he said, pinching her cheek. "You'll probably keep on growing like a stump for a year or two then shoot up into a big ole Amazon woman."

She glared up at him and frowned.

"Look, kid," he said, laying his hand on the back of her head. "I think I kind of know how you feel. But if all you got to worry about is being a little pip-squeak in a hurry to grow up, well, in these hard times, that's doing pretty good, huh?"

"Yeah."

"And you know what? Remember I told you they got all kinds of people at those circus and sideshow places. But you know who're the most talented, smartest, and cutest girls at the carnivals?"

"Who?"

"The midgets."

"Really?"

"Shoot, yeah! Had me a girl at a sideshow one time," he said, and she felt a little twinge of something right under her heart that she'd never felt before. "Stage name was Tiny Tina. Ain't never been a cuter sight in this world than her riding around the ring on her miniature white horse. She could sing and dance, did a little tap-dance act. Wore one of them big Mexican sombrero hats, looked like a little ole toadstool tap dancing. Everybody in the circus, from the fat lady to the trapeze man, looked up to her. You know how come?"

"How come?"

"Because she was a feisty little thing, proud of who she was, held her head high, that's how come. Always remember, kid: You're only as tall as you stand."

Lovesick

Much of what happened the next two or three days remained in Trixie's memory like clippings for a collage, like snapshots laid out in a loose arrangement, not affixed to the pages, out of sequence and easily altered and rearranged decades later as she mulled over them. She recalled a Sunday morning spent at the little Episcopal Church of the Transfiguration that sat on a hilltop above Saluda like a small, lavishly frosted wedding cake in the snow. Ollie Pearl and the Colonel had gone too, she remembered. Dovie Blackburn and Naomi? She thought so. Edna, definitely. Even Frank—looking handsome, she'd give him that much, in his Sunday-go-to-meeting suit. She went another time, too. Was she alone? She couldn't remember. Did she dream it? Maybe. But she had wanted to see it empty—its dark, woodsy, and faerie-fanciful interior with sharp-pointed doors and windows. The unnameable, magical something she sensed in the laurel woods and by the creek loitered there when the little sanctuary was empty. Of that she was sure.

But most memories centered around Laurel Terrace all decked out for Christmas, the damp, deep-earth-scented laurel woods, and, mostly, Joe's sad little camp by the tracks, from which she couldn't stay away. She recalled the crafty ways she came up with to avoid discovery. She would volunteer to go to the henhouse, taking two or three hours to bring back the eggs.

"Where's Trixie?"

"Gone to the henhouse for eggs," Naomi would say.

Trixie moved in on the children playing in the Wilcoxes' yard, playing a game of tag with them before sneaking away to Joe's camp.

"What have you been up to this afternoon, Trixie?"

"Playing tag with those girls next door."

Edna had kept her hands wiped clean of her. If Ollie Pearl expressed concerns about Trixie's whereabouts and activities, those concerns, once spoken, seemed to float away like feathers, thanks to the attention the Colonel paid Ollie Pearl, to Ollie Pearl's spoken trust of Trixie, and to Ollie Pearl's faith that Naomi wouldn't let her go too far or get into too much trouble.

Joe had taken her on a guided tour through the few tents and tar-paper shacks of the hobo jungle. They shared some of Naomi's eats with Scoop Shovel and a 'bo named Hard Luck Larry. One day they walked along the tracks to Saluda. Knowing she ought not to let anyone see her with Joe, they went their separate ways before they arrived in town. On that day Joe got two hours' worth of work washing dishes at Ward's Grill while she hung out at Pace's and chatted with Esther. In between customers, Trixie watched Esther put apple-red polish on her long fingernails or take delicate nibbles from the slice of fruitcake Trixie had brought her from the inn. Nearly everything Joe had told Trixie, she told Esther in spurts of excited babbling that made Esther smile. Esther knew of Jungle Buzzard, she said. Jimmy Ray, she called him. He had lived there all his life and had left to go hoboing so his family would have one less mouth to feed. They watched from the window inside the store while Joe, with Boy at his side, charmed passengers getting on and off the train, trying to sell them strings of the few chinquapins he'd found in the woods. "Ten cents for a string, three for a quarter, one for your wife and two for your daughter!"

She had always known that every passing hour brought her closer to the day Hobo Joe would leave. And even if for some reason he didn't, she herself would have to leave for Five Forks after the first of the year. So, one day, while at Pace's Store buying Edna some Sal Hepatica, she shared the depth of her heartache with Esther, who listened a long time, smiling but sad-eyed and understanding.

Trixie looked forlornly at the bottle and said she sure wished Sal Hepatica would help her condition.

"Oh, no!" Esther cried out, her tinkling laughter turning heads in the store. She took the bottle from Trixie's hand and showed her the label where it claimed the mixture, when added to water, had the same laxative effect as the natural mineral waters of Bohemia. "I don't think a laxative is what you need, sugar!" Esther said. "But maybe Madame Phoebia Sullivan could help you. They say she makes a special love potion!"

So Trixie, holding on to the little bit of change left over from the purchase, followed Esther's directions to Madame Sullivan's shanty in the woods.

Madame Sullivan, in a white dress and turban that made her face look dark as a coffee bean, sat next to a small table with a soup bowl and spoon and a pile of letters. She nodded as Trixie eased the screen door shut behind her. She shuffled in her chair and lay her hands on her belly and raised her chin, not smiling. She asked Trixie her troubles and Trixie explained. Madame Sullivan smiled. She asked how much money she had, and Trixie dug deep into her coat pocket and held out the dime and few pennies.

Madame Sullivan pointed to the smallest bottle, a tiny red one, among a shelf filled with jars and colored bottles of her cleansing teas and potions. Trixie took it from the shelf and looked at it doubtfully.

"If you believe it will work, it will work," Madame Sullivan said.

"How long will it take?"

"It will work the moment you drink it, if you have faith it will work." She watched as Trixie turned up the bottle and sipped the bottle dry. "You feel better now," Madame Sullivan said, a statement not a question.

"I think I do!"

Madame Sullivan nodded and smiled her knowing smile.

Trixie stepped sprite-like through the crystal woods and found her way to the creek, truly feeling lighter of spirit, until she approached Bo Joe's camp. She stopped when she saw him flinging off his shoes and socks and rolling up his britches to the knees, with the dog at his side, watching. She kept her distance and watched him take the towel and soap from the line and over to the fire, where he'd poured creek water into the tin tub to warm. He threw his hat and shirt on a laurel bush. He knelt at the tub, dipped a tin can into it, and dumped water over his head, gasping in the cold air. It made Trixie hurt to watch, and she saw something sorrowful in the working of his arms and shoulders, as, still gasping, he hurriedly ran the bar of soap all over his head, face, neck, and torso. He washed his feet. He lathered up and doused himself with a tin can of water again and again.

He grabbed the towel and rubbed himself from head to waist. Shivering, he put on his shirt and sweater and crouched by the fire, rubbing his hands together, and shivered some more. "How about a bath, Boy?" she heard him ask the dog as she eased through the woods a little closer to them. "Can't get the girls if you stink, don't you know." He scratched the dog's chest, cupped the floppy jaws in his hands, let Boy lick him in the face—"loving him up" a whole lot more than he'd ever let Trixie see him do.

Trixie waited a while then strolled down to the creek and over the bridge. Joe had picked up the nugget of wood and was scraping fine lines around its eyes.

"Oh, hey there, kid. You just missed yourself a show." The face had now started to 'come up' out of it, he told her. He made two vertical tracks between the eyebrows.

"Why are you doing that to him?" she asked. "You're making him look old!"

"He's feeling old. He's got himself some worries."

Trixie then began to realize that Joe put as much of himself in his handiwork as he brought out of it. "What kind of worries?"

He shook his head.

She knelt beside him and grabbed his arm. "Joe, I've been thinking."

He grinned and tapped her forehead. "Uh-oh!"

"I want to catch out a freight."

"What? You? Shoot! A little squirt like you? Huh-uh."

"How come?"

"It's dangerous, that's how come."

But a little while later they heard a train crawling—*cuh-lunk, cuh-lunk*—along the tracks. She pulled at his arm. "Please!"

He let out a long sigh and shook his head. "Well, come on then," he said. "This one's hardly moving at all—a 'drag' is what the 'boes call it—and we'll just go a little ways up the track. But you can still get hurt, so watch me and be real careful.

"What a regular 'bo does, if he's catching out on the fly—that's hopping a train that's moving at some speed—is run until he's running at the same speed as the train. That part's not hard, slow as this one's moving—we call this 'pickin' up a drag'—then he'll reach up with his right hand and take hold of the grab bar at the front of the car, not at the back, hold on tight, hold on tight. That's the way a real 'bo does it, but what you're going to do is watch me. Then I'm going to grab your hand and pull you up."

Though the train crawled along as if it would stop at any time, she still had to make many steps to his one. But he hopped on first and reached down and pulled her up into the boxcar. The dog followed along for a while—*Woof! Woof! Woof!*—then sat on his haunches in the middle of the track, looking smaller and more pitiful with the distance.

"We'll be back, Boy!" Trixie cried out.

Later, riding along, hugging her knees to her chest, she decided that the hobo's life would suit her just fine. With Hobo Joe by her side, she could withstand any misfortune that might come her way.

While they rode, slowly, *cuh-lunk, cuh-lunk*, Joe told her how he used to wrap his belt around the rail of the catwalk at the top of the boxcars and idle that way all night, moonrise to moonset, "chasing the moon," he called it. He'd watch the stars come out like little pins on a piece of black velvet. He'd seen meteor showers like salt pouring out of a shaker.

"After a while you get pictures burned in your mind," he said, "the lights inside the living rooms of houses and in little whistle-stop cafés you pass, an old graveyard lit up by the moon. One time I lay awake all night on top of a coal car while it chased the moon across the prairies." He looked up at the sky, and she did, too, as if this was the first time she'd seen it, and in a way it was. "I think we'll have us a big ole full one tonight," he said.

A short while and maybe a mile or so up the track, they hopped off the freight and took a slow walk back to Joe's camp. By the time they reached it, the day's light had dimmed above the treetops and deep shade had settled between the tree trunks. The dog loped along behind them, tail and tongue wagging, pleased at their reunion.

"That was fun," Trixie said. "I want to do it again."

"No way. It's dangerous, like I told you." Joe poked in the fire he'd just started, trying to get it going good. "Speaking of dangerous, don't you think you ought to be getting on home now? You show up after dark, you'll be in a whole heap of trouble, and I might, too. They might lock you up in the attic and send the law after me."

"Can't I stay just a little bit longer?"

"Well, suit yourself. I reckon since there's a full moon coming up, once you do start back you'll be able to see anybody—or anything—you might happen to meet up with in the woods, in time to run from it."

"What do you mean 'anything'? Like what?"

He shrugged. "Oh, you know, like haints or boogers. I hear tell the Appalachian Mountain Woolly-Winged Wood Boogers are your worst. Don't worry, though. I reckon if one of 'em was to grab you"—his hand shot out and he grabbed her by the arm, making her squeal—"you can holler like you just did and maybe . . . maybe . . . I can run fast enough to save you before the booger runs off with you clenched in its jaws."

"There's no such thing as haints and boogers!"

When she still made no move to leave, he sat a while, looking into the burning embers, firelight making quick-shifting shadows on his face.

"What are you thinking?" she asked.

"Thinking about the night I came here. . . ." He shook his head, let his voice fall two notches lower. "I was coming up this way from Georgia. I'd caught a local outside of Spartanburg, had an empty car all to myself. Cold, almost clear night, moon flying through raggy black clouds. Felt like a blame fool heading north in the winter, but Jungle Buzzard gave me wind of some piddling work he'd heard about here, had let me in on these fine accommodations. Well, I'd just caught that freight on the fly, was still hanging on just inside the door—car was squeakin' and groanin' and slingin' me this way and that way, so I had to hold on for my life—when down by the track I caught sight of another 'bo trottin' by the side, skinny little bugger, running hell for leather. Train was picking up too much speed by then; he was having a heck of a time keeping up. I knew it might cost me to give him a hand, might get him and me both sliced and diced. "Give it up, 'bo!" I hollered. "Catch the next one out! Go on!"

"'Help me! Help me!' he hollered back. Now, that by itself made my skin crawl. That don't sound like hobo talk. His voice had a high pitch to it, too, more of a scream than a holler. I'd no sooner finished thinking that thought when his cap blew off and let fly a head of long, wild hair!"

"He was a girl!"

"You got that right. White face with eyes big and wild and bleary looking. Well, I was white-knuckling with my right hand and reaching down to her with my left, the wind beatin' up my face and head. My fingers, I stretched 'em so long and hard, felt like my knuckles was comin' undone! Just as quick as I grabbed ahold of her hand, I wished I hadn't done it. I'm ashamed to tell you that I let out my own scream then—a real bloodcurdler!"

"How come?!"

"That hand, that's how come. I'll never forget the feel of that hand."

He slowly shook his head, turned it slowly, and looked at her. She read pure terror in his eyes.

"Now, it was a cold night, just like this one, but that hand, I tell you what. . . ."

"What?"

"Ain't no better way to tell you how cold that hand was except to say it was all I could do, all I could do, not to shake it off. And the only reason I didn't was, it flashed through my mind what had happened to Uncle Hard Times. I couldn't do it, couldn't let her loose to get mushed under the wheels. I clamped my teeth shut, held on, and hoisted her up into the car and helped her fall toward the far back corner. I sat down across the car from her. A block of moonlight lay on the floor between us, but I tell you, it was so dark back in that corner where she was, her white face was just a smear of light. She wasn't much for volunteer talking, so I asked her, 'Where you headed, 'bo?' and, after I'd asked her again, she finally answered, her voice so low I could hardly hear it above the *cah-lumph cah-lumph* of the car against the rails. She was hopping off at Melrose Junction and heading to Green Creek, she said. 'You heard tell there's work there?' I asked her. She just looked up at me then, big eyes a-blazin'. Didn't say a word. Well, there's some 'boes who play their cards close to their chest; there's not much work, so they hear tell there's work somewhere, they know better than to talk it up. Something about that blaze in her eyes, I didn't ask her twice. She laid her head down on her knees and with that white face out of sight, that cold corner went dark as the grave, cold and deep and dark as the grave. . . ." He trailed off and fell quiet.

Trixie pulled on his arm. "What happened then?"

"Well, a while later we pulled into Melrose, and I started to stand up, aiming to give her a hand down, but she was gone—just gone! Didn't take me long to figure out I was onto a mystery."

"What did you do?"

"I hopped off there at Melrose and walked around and asked around till I found that Green Creek. Wasn't much to it but a crossroads of two old roadbeds with a faded old sign on a boarded up store that said 'Green Creek.' A no-dog town. One dim light on the porch of one house. I knocked on the door, and a haggard looking woman opened it. 'That's my daughter, Nellie, you're talking about,' she said when I told her my tale. She showed me a picture, and I swear it was the selfsame girl as that 'bo I'd help hop the freight. She showed me something else, too. A postcard Nellie had sent her sometime back. *I'm comin' home, Mama,* it said. *I'm done a-wanderin'.*

"'She died three years ago this very night,' her mama said. 'She was killed while catching a freight a few miles down the track.'

"'That can't be!' I said to her. 'It just can't be!'

"'Young man,' she said to me then, 'you are not the first one to come here and tell me you have seen her, so I stay here in this no-dog town and keep on this one dim porch light in this one little house, hoping that one day she will make it back.'

"Well," Joe said to Trixie, "I reckon she's still a-wanderin', that Nellie, still tryin' to make her way home. . . . Wish she'd get there and stay put! One night, I swear to you, I was sittin' by the fire here when I felt a cold, cold hand on the back of my neck. . . ."

Trixie shook off a shiver as Joe's voice trailed off. She sat there a minute, wide-eyed, then jumped up. "I guess I'd better go now. Like you said, I'll be in big trouble if I get home after dark." She took off toward the bridge over the creek.

"Hey, don't you want me to tell you about the night I saw the ghost of Lincoln's funeral train?" she heard him call out, laughing. "Flatcar behind the casket had a whole orchestra of skeletons glowin' in the dark, playin' a long, mournful dirge. . . ." But she was halfway across the bridge by then.

Good-byes

The days that came afterward looked like the winter scenes on Edna's blue-and-white Currier & Ives plates, which became familiar to Trixie since one of her chores was to lay them out on the dining room table before supper. The sky, like the sky in those scenes, looked too blue to be true; snow covered the rooftops and filigreed the trees. Rafe and Frank cut down a big fir tree and put it up in the corner by the radio in the parlor.

Esther came to visit, and she helped Trixie hang the garland she'd made from pages of the Sears-Roebuck catalog and the silver stars she'd made from the lining of cigarette packages. Esther and Trixie gathered up some of the dark green ivy that grew on a shaded bank near the well house. Together they draped the doorways and the mantel of the old stone fireplace with the ivy. All the while, Esther chattered happily about what she could do with the marvelous old house if it were hers. It could become a mansion, almost!

Frank kept standing in the doorway, eyeing Esther. He brought in a ladder and offered to help put up the greenery over the tall entryway to the dining room. Frank sent Trixie to the kitchen to ask Naomi for some thumbtacks, and she came back just in time to see Esther smack him on the face for some reason or another.

Later, Trixie stood on a stool over the pastry table while Esther showed her how to stud apples with cloves and then dip them in cinnamon and nutmeg. "When they dry, they'll shrivel up and become as light as feathers, almost," Esther said. "You'll see!" Pomanders, Esther called them. You could hang them on the Christmas tree or put them in your closet to make your clothes smell like Christmas for months to come. Later that day Trixie sat at the edge of her bed, legs dangling, letting Esther stroke her toenails with pale pink enamel.

Anybody looking in a window one of those nights before Christmas might have seen Naomi fussing around in the kitchen and Trixie sitting on a stool not far from her, polishing the silver for Christmas Day dinner, stitching together a little pouch out of muslin for a gift for Joe, or stringing buttons together with embroidery thread to make a bracelet for Esther. In the parlor the others' faces gave back the light of the fire. Dovie, Ollie Pearl, and Edna made needlework ornaments or quilted pillows, the kind of things you gave as gifts back then. Nobody had a lot to give and nobody expected a lot.

Old Jack sat at his station in front of the radio, twisting the knob, dodging the static so they could all hear "Lux Radio Theater" or Bing Crosby singing on Chesterfield's "Music that Satisfies." The Colonel was there, too, sitting up straight as a store mannequin, never far from Ollie Pearl. On Jack Benny night Frank lay flat on his back on the floor, his cigarette adding to the haze of smoke that nobody thought a thing in the world about in those days.

One of those nights she slipped up to Frank's room and pawed through the clothes in his bureau drawers in hopes of finding some smaller clothes he or his older brothers had worn when they were younger. No luck there, but she knew no one got rid of things back then. Inspiration: the alcove at the end of the hallway where Edna stored everything useful though no longer used. There Trixie had no trouble finding and snitching a shirt and pair of britches among piles of them that Edna's three boys had worn when young. She held them against her and found the pants legs and sleeves too long, but not by too much. She found a cap, too, and, eventually, after a lot of digging around, a little coat! She smuggled them into her room and hid them under her bed. She robbed a quilt from the closet and rolled it up. What to secure the bindle with? Back to Frank's room for his belt, the one he wore with his Sunday-go-to-meeting suit.

In the empty hallway, but mostly in her mind, she rehearsed running beside the train, running hell for leather! *Run! Run until you match the speed of the train! Reach up with your right hand and take the grab bar at the front of the car, not at the back, front not back, hold on tight, hold on tight!* "That's the way a real 'bo does it," he had told her, "when they're catching out a freight on the fly."

Still, she hoped for a "drag" like the one they'd picked up that day. "What you're going to do is watch me," he'd said before they ran for the slow-moving freight. "Then I'm going to grab your hand." If Joe hadn't refused to grab poor Wanderin' Nellie's hand to pull her up to safety, he surely wouldn't refuse her, would he?

She was more than ready to see what was around the bend, to chase the moon with Bo Joe. Only one thing held her back—the thought of breaking Ollie Pearl's heart. But then she overheard Edna, speaking of Ollie Pearl and the Colonel, say to Naomi, "Mark my word, there'll be wedding bells ringing after the first of the year." Those words lodged in Trixie's mind, confirming what she ought to have expected. Ollie Pearl's husband, Jarvis, hadn't wanted a child to raise; would the Colonel really want to, when it came down to it?

After dinner the night of Christmas Eve, Ollie Pearl read the Christmas story. She held on her lap the big Bible that had belonged to Jarvis's and Edna's grandfather, and she opened it to the second chapter of Luke. "And it came to pass in those days. . . ," she began.

All the while, in her mind, Trixie already sat on the porch, her chin cupped in her hands, waiting for the next one who might take her in. Who?

Who who who? she heard, later that night. She sat up in bed. An owl? *Who who who?* A thump at the French door. Trixie jumped out of bed and pulled the bedspread around her like a cloak. She pressed her nose to the frosty glass. A snowball had hit and splattered. She eased the door open and stepped out.

"Hey!"

She turned her head toward a shadow next to the shadow cast by the spruce. Joe tipped his hat. Boy loped up behind him. Red and Blue came running, barking. He shushed the three dogs, who then contented themselves with sniffing each other down. She hung over the terrace wall.

"I'm looking at heading out tonight!" he called up in a loud whisper. "Just wanted to tell you—"

"Tonight? No! Don't! Wait!"

Ollie Pearl popped up in bed. "What're you doing, Trixie? Who're you talking to? Get in out of the cold! And shut the door! This minute!" When Trixie came back in, Ollie Pearl said, "What were you doing out there, Trixie? What was it? Who was it?"

"Nobody. A bird hit the window, that's all."

Ollie Pearl sighed, got out of bed, and put on her robe. "Oh, dear me. When a bird hits the window, somebody's going to die soon. I've always heard it. I'll not sleep the rest of the night for worrying over who!" She switched on the light at her desk and started writing letters.

Trixie fell back in bed and covered her head with the blanket. *It's going to be me. Might as well be me.*

When the train whistle blew at midnight, its whine seemed to go on and on.

"See there!" Ollie Pearl said, looking up from her letters when she heard Trixie's sniffling. "You've already caught your death of cold!"

That next morning, early on Christmas Day, Trixie sneaked downstairs and out of the house, even before Naomi arrived. She'd pocketed the gift she had made Joe and put together a lump from some side meat and cold biscuits, in case she found him still there. Would he be there? The sun had just come up, and the trees glittered with sparkles of red when she started out on the loneliest walk of her life, or so she thought then. Down by the creek, the snow had blown from the trees and had cast a loose drape over the snow 'bo, which now looked like a snowman's ghost.

She would always remember the elation welling up inside her when she found Joe sitting by his campfire, shoulders hunched over with the cold. And she'd also remember how her joy diminished when she didn't see the dog anywhere around. Had Joe issued Boy his walking papers? She watched the slow, tired way Joe picked up a rock and tossed it into the icy creek. He reached in his pocket and pulled out his pocketknife and the piece of wood and started in on it. She crept closer, found a rock, and tossed it—*plop!*—into the creek.

Joe looked up. "Oh, hey there, kid."

Trixie sat down beside him with her arms locked around her knees. She watched as he added more lines and notches on the figure's face. "What're you doing to it now?"

"Just finishing him up. And studying over something."

"About leaving, I guess? I was scared you'd be gone already."

"Almost was. Came to tell you."

"I couldn't come out. She wouldn't let me."

"Yeah, I should've known. Dumb of me to try it."

The dog still hadn't shown up. "Where'd Boy go?"

"I run him off. Gave him his official notice last night. Told him he'd have to find him another gravy train to ride. Best me and him made a clean break." He sliced his hand sideways through the air when he said it.

"Look, there he is!" Trixie said a few minutes later, when she spotted Boy a few yards away, ears drooped, slouching their way. He gave one hopeful wag of his tail.

"Go on, Boy! Git!" Joe yelled, and the dog dropped to the ground, chin resting on his forepaws. "He don't like it, but he'll be all right. He'll either get on up the road or take right up with whoever takes over this spot right here, maybe Scoop Shovel Sam, if I can't get Scoop to go with me."

"I guess you're going pretty soon, huh?"

"Yeah. J. B. himself brought me some news. He drops by at Christmas to hand over to his mama anything he earned. Said there're a couple of tankers that need some men down in Tampa. Sounds like a real good deal, even before you ship out. You can stay there a couple of weeks while they train you, and they feed you pretty good, too. That's what I wanted to tell you last night. Wasn't so sure you'd be down here today, it being Christmas and all. I'm headed out tonight, for sure."

She could see all the miles and miles of railroad track that would stretch on and on between them. Then all that ocean. And all the years. Worst of all, the years. "Do you really have to leave, Bo Joe?"

He tied the strings of her hood under her chin. "You stick that lip back in, now. I've been telling you all along, from the very first day, that what a hobo does is go. Got to go where I hear there's some work. Gotta work, gotta eat."

"But—"

"Ain't no buts about it. Man's got some pride, don't you know. Can't stay around here bumming food off his little gal friend."

Little gal friend, he said!

They were quiet for a while. She sniffled.

"You're not going to go to blubberin' all over the place, are you?"

She didn't look up at him. "No. Ollie Pearl said I'm catching cold." She handed him the lump. "Here, Naomi would want you to have this. I brought you a present, too. It's a little pouch for your coins and your gold nuggets and glass eye and things."

"Hey, thanks, kid. Look at it! You did this all by yourself?"

She nodded, pleased he was so pleased.

"It's real well made," he said. "Got a drawstring and everything." He drew it tight with the drawstring then opened it again, like he'd never seen anything like it before. He walked over to the boxcar and got his bindle. He sat next to her again, unwrapped it, and took out his treasures. He put each coin, each marble, each little chunk of gold, the gold tooth, and the glass eye into the small sack. Then he drew the string tight and looped it around his belt. "Won't I be something? Some bum tries to steal my valuables, he'll have to kill me first. Thanks, kid."

The sun had come up. The sparkles from the trees, all clear and colorless now, hurt her eyes.

"Here's what I've got to give you," he said, holding the wooden piece so she could see it. "It took me a long time because there was something in its eyes that I couldn't get to come up. Finally got it right, I think. And I put a notch at the top of it so you can hang it on your Christmas tree someday." He blew the dust off of it, wiped the sawdust clear with his thumb, and looked it over. He laid it in the palm of her hand.

She held it there and looked at it for a long time, at the long and narrow face, the wild and wavy beard. Creases fine as hairs lined the eyes, which looked wise and watchful. And teasing. Lovingly teasing.

"That's me when I'm a real, real old man," he said. "Skinny, all wrinkled-up, beard down to my belly button, walking around bent over double, holding myself up with a walking stick."

"Thanks, Bo Joe. I like it a lot. I'll keep it always." She didn't say anything else for a while.

"What's going through your little head?"

"I was just wondering, what if you miss the midnight freight tonight?"

"Then I'll just catch the next one out."

"Oh. Well, suppose you missed the freight tonight but caught the one tomorrow, made it all the way to Florida, and found out you missed the ship?"

"Don't know. Might stay down there in Florida if I could find work. Far sight warmer down there than here."

"Maybe you could come back here?"

"Nah, no work here. Besides, I'm the kind of 'bo who don't plow the same ground twice."

"You know what, Bo Joe? You and me, we're both orphans, kind of. We both of us don't ever know where we're going to end up. We're a lot alike."

"Yeah," he said. "We're two regular Joes, ain't we? You and me, kid, we're two peas in a pod. You better head on home now. It's Christmas, and they'll be getting up early. Come on, I'll walk you back up to the house."

They crossed the creek and entered the long green tunnel. "Joe," she said, "wonder if we might see each other again, some way, somehow?"

"I wouldn't count on it, kid."

"Maybe when you're a real, real old man, all wrinkled up with a long beard down to your navel?"

He laughed. "You'd be a little old woman by then, all shriveled up like a dried apple doll!"

"But I wouldn't care!"

"No, I wouldn't either."

"Where my aunt lives, right in town in Five Forks, 304 Devonshire, it's not far from the railroad tracks. Will you remember it, I mean, just in case you're riding the rails and you pass that way? 304 Devonshire. Just in case?"

"Yeah, I'll remember." He lifted her high up on his shoulders, so high that she reached up and shook the branches, showering snow down on their heads. "Hey!" he cried out.

They walked on until they'd come near the end of the path. Just around the bend, she could see Naomi in the kitchen, leaning over the open door of the woodstove. Joe dropped her down from his shoulders. He reached down and tweaked her nose, then her chin.

"You better hurry," he said. "They'll be missing you soon."

"Joe, remember you said you knew girl hoboes?"

"Don't even get started thinking that way, kid. Hoboing's a mighty hard life. It's something you do because you have to, not because you want to." He took her hands in his and pulled at her fingers under the mittens. "Those little monkey hands couldn't even grab onto a tender. Besides it wouldn't be right, you a kid and me practically a grown-up and all."

"But you're not but three years older than me!"

"That three years is like ten. One day you'll know what I mean."

"If I had been, say, almost fifteen and you'd been eighteen, maybe then it would have been different?"

"Might have been, kid. Might have been."

Blackberry Summer

Trixie had a plan, and only because of it did she manage to part with Joe and get through Christmas Day. Santa Claus didn't come to town—Trixie was, after all, almost twelve years old—but they had a fine Christmas Day. They had the last of the corn and yams and turnip greens Naomi had put up. They still had a ham off of the hog Rafe had killed in November. They had Naomi's chocolate Yule log and fruitcake and tall stack cake that had dried apples mixed with molasses between the thin layers. The women of the house gave each other gifts of lace handkerchiefs and cathedral-windows pillow covers. The men received cigars, cigarette lighters, and pipe tobacco. Frank liked his new rifle and the five-flavor pound cake Naomi had made for him.

Though she felt she'd outgrown dolls of any kind, Trixie thanked Dovie and Effie for her Shirley Temple paper dolls. She shared them with Effie, who'd yanked them out of Trixie's hands when she opened them, wanting to keep them for herself. She cut out the clothes with scissors and let Effie affix the small white tabs of the paper dresses to Shirley's shoulders. When Trixie opened the Cashmere Bouquet perfumed soap Esther had given her, she held it up to her face and breathed deep of it, thinking it would come in handy in her new life on the road.

Everybody acted pleased with the pomanders Trixie gave them—everybody except Frank, who turned up his nose at his. "Stinks!" he said. Edna opened a box of Whitman's chocolates from her sons in West Virginia and cried.

Afterwards, they all gathered around the piano and sang every carol that Dovie could play and a lot she couldn't, then most of them sat around the radio and listened to Lionel Barrymore play Ebenezer Scrooge.

Ollie Pearl stayed up late again that night writing letters, something she'd never done until the night before.

Why this night? This night of all nights! Trixie lay in bed, pretending to sleep, her heart thumping, one eye peeping out from under the covers, watching the soft glow on her aunt's smiling face in the lamplight. Hinting to her correspondents about those wedding bells, no doubt. *Go to bed!* Trixie had an idea. She sat up in bed, rubbed her eyes, and grumbled.

"Having trouble sleeping, sugar?" Ollie Pearl asked, as Trixie had hoped she would. "Is it the light? Oh, I'm sorry." But before she switched off the light, she stepped over to Trixie's bedside, took her hand, and gently, with much unnecessary buildup beforehand, announced her plans to marry the Colonel. "We're both of some age," she said, "and we've recently received news about his health. We might not have many years together, but—"

"I hope you'll be very happy with the Colonel, Aunt Ollie," Trixie said, much too fast.

"Not only me, Trixie!" she declared, patting her hand. "You too!"

When Ollie Pearl finally switched off the lamp, Trixie lay under the covers, swallowing hard, waiting. Barely a few minutes before midnight, she peeped over and saw Ollie Pearl's shoulders rising and falling in the moonlight that beamed through the frosty glass door. She pulled Frank's boyhood clothes out from under the bed. She slipped on the britches and shirt, turned up the legs and sleeves once or twice. The coat sleeves hung down to her knuckles. She piled up her hair and secured it with bobby pins from Ollie Pearl's dressing table. She put on the cap, which dropped to her eyebrows and half covered her ears. She tiptoed to the writing desk and scribbled a note on a piece of Ollie Pearl's white embossed stationery, saying "I'll write." She picked up her bindle, swung it over her shoulder, and eased out the door, praying the door didn't squeak and that Red and Blue hadn't wandered into the backyard from their sleeping places on the front porch. A gust of cold air rushed into the room, and Ollie Pearl stirred and pulled the covers up over her shoulders.

What would poor Ollie Pearl think if she woke up and saw a boy standing at the door, then opened her eyes wider and saw Trixie dressed up as a boy? What would such a sight do to her mind? What if she died from the shock of it? Trixie held her breath and watched through the cold haze of glass until Ollie Pearl stayed still for a full moment. *Good-bye, dear sweet Aunt Ollie Pearl! Thank you for everything! I'll write! I really will, I promise!*

Her footsteps cushioned by the snow, Trixie stepped across the backyard without awaking Red and Blue. The moon shone over the once smooth field of snow that her footprints had disfigured over many days. She looked back at the old house, at the moonlight reflecting in the windows. *Good-bye, Naomi! Good-bye, warm, heaven-scented kitchen!*

She had started down the path when the whistle blew. *Run! Run!* She heard the slow then faster *chug-chug-chug-chug* of the train gaining momentum going down the grade. *Hurry!* Her chest burned as she sucked in the cold air. She ran, her feet pounding the ground, faster, faster. *Run! Run until you match the speed of the train! Reach up with your right hand and take the grab bar at the front of the car, not at the back, front not back, hold on tight, hold on tight!*

But when she reached the bridge over the creek, she stopped, panting, chest heaving. The whistle blew again, and the freight *chuff-chuff-chuff-chuffed* on its way. She stood at the edge of the creek, hands to her knees, breathing hard, crying hard, then laughing with relief when she saw the fire in the stone circle near the boxcar, burning low, but still burning. "Hey!" she called out. She scrambled over the bridge. "Hey!"

"Woof! Woof woof!"

"Hey!" Her word came out as a scream. "Hey, Boy! Hey, Bo Joe!" But as she neared the campfire, she could see Scoop Shovel Sam's lined face and bleary eyes looking back at her, hanging onto the scruff of Boy's neck, holding him back.

All along the path back to the house, Trixie walked slowly, thinking of the miles and miles of distance piling up in the wake of the whistle. The lonesome drone of the train hung on and on and on in the air, and when it finally died away, she felt as if a whole continent stretched out between her and Bo Joe.

She would always remember the way Ollie Pearl looked when she shot up in the bed that night. Unloosed pin curls sprung like bedspring coils from her head. She sat up, holding the covers over her bosom, her bare, bony feet dangling like a dead chicken's off the side of the bed.

"Who are you?" Ollie Pearl screamed. "What are you doing in this room?" But worse, far worse, when Trixie took off her cap and let her hair fall over her red, tear-splotched face, Ollie Pearl's mouth gaped wide open like a baby bird's. Her eyes stared out, stunned at the sight of Trixie, who stood right in front of her in a boy's clothes.

"Why, Trixie! Oh!" she said. "Oh, no! Oh, my goodness! Oh, my land!" She sucked in her breath, hard. She covered her face with her hands and peeped out between her fingers like a child. "I don't understand! I'm just mortified, just mortified!" she kept saying, as Trixie, sobbing, threw herself on her bed.

Ollie Pearl married the Colonel that spring, and he had preferred his house in China Grove to Ollie Pearl's on Devonshire Street in Five Forks. Trixie remembered the months that followed as Blackberry Summer because she spent hours picking blackberries at the railroad tracks a half mile or so from the house where they had moved. She'd walk along the track, a mile or so north then back, a mile or so south then back, slowly, slowly, hoping a train would pass. The heat burned the back of her neck, and ticks crawled on her shirt sleeves and pants legs.

Every once in a while she'd look up and hold her hand over her eyes against the sun. She'd look down the long track to where the heat waved, right at the spot where the two steel rails came together at the bend, and sometimes she'd see somebody with a bindle swung over his shoulder walking her way, tipping his hat, waving, melting into the air just before she came close enough to see his face. It didn't fool her after the first time, though. She knew Bo Joe couldn't know where they'd moved. Could he?

Ollie Pearl would stand by the door of the room where Trixie lay on the bed with her back to the door and her head on her outstretched arm, staring out the window. Ollie Pearl would put a cold washcloth on Trixie's forehead and would shake her head. "Heaven, help me. Why in this world did I ever think I could raise a young girl?

"Please, Trixie," she'd say and finger Trixie's hair, then throw her hands up, then wander back to the kitchen, where Trixie would hear her whispering to the Colonel.

"It will pass, Olivia," she would hear him say, in a voice grown weak and ragged with illness. "All things do, in time."

Pearl Harbor

The Christmas of 1940 came, and Ollie Pearl said, "Well, Trixie, I guess we'll go on up to Edna's." They hadn't gone much at all while the Colonel was living, but earlier that year he had died, and a getaway visit to Laurel Terrace seemed the right thing to do. They had other reasons. Edna had just had a gallstone removed, and Ollie Pearl had in her mind she ought to be there. Frank had enlisted in the Navy and had come home on leave. They'd have a chance to see him, too, not that Trixie cared one way or another. Ollie Pearl had badgered Trixie into writing him a letter after he enlisted, and afterward Frank had sent her a cute charm bracelet with the Capitol building and the Lincoln and Jefferson memorials on it from Washington, D.C. Ollie Pearl had insisted she write him thank-you letters every time he sent something, so, in time, a little civility, if not affection, grew between them.

When Frank, twenty by then, met them at the station, he had his sailor hat cocked sideways on his head. Still all teeth, but good-looking, yes.

"Isn't he a handsome thing?" Ollie Pearl whispered to her, and Trixie had to admit he was.

He sized Trixie up head to toe before he even blinked once. Trixie, who would turn seventeen that April, had filled out some in the right places and had learned to smile with her lips closed to hide the gap in her teeth, which hadn't grown together as Joe had promised. Frank raised his eyebrows, picked his cigarette out of his mouth, twisted it out with the toe of his foot, and draped his arm around her, all in one motion, it seemed.

"Well, how's my little pen pal?" he said.

Before the ride to Laurel Terrace in the new Plymouth, Ollie Pearl helped Edna, still recovering from her gallbladder operation, into the backseat. Ollie Pearl hustled to sit in the back with her. "You young people sit up front together," she said. "You've probably got so much to talk about."

Trixie sighed and rolled her eyes, but she obliged.

"He reminds me of Jarvis right across the eyes, doesn't he you, Edna?" Ollie Pearl said.

"Yes, but everybody says the mouth and teeth are pure Clark Gable."

"You're glad to be home on leave, I guess, Frank," Trixie said. Well, she had to say something to him as they rode along.

"Glad to be back, gladder to head out again." He had another cigarette in his fingers by that time and had his wrist lopped across the steering wheel while he drove with one hand.

"Oh, and why is that?"

"You ever heard the saying 'Ignorance is bliss'? Until I left these hills, I didn't know what a damn hillbilly backwater this place was."

A short while later, they arrived at Laurel Terrace, and Frank carried in their suitcases. The Blackburn sisters had moved away, Ollie Pearl had told Trixie beforehand; Dovie had married one of the Pace men and had taken Effie to live with her out in the county somewhere. But Old Jack greeted them when they entered the parlor.

He looked even rounder in his blue pin-striped overalls, and his eyes looked a bit filmier. "What in tarnation?" he said, squinting when he saw Trixie, letting her hug him before he went back to his radio.

"Come now and visit 79 Wistful Vista with Fibber McGee and Molly!" a voice blurted from the radio.

Ollie Pearl helped Edna into an easy chair. "I know you wanted to go with Frank to meet us," Ollie Pearl told Edna, "but you ought to have stayed put."

Trixie ran to the kitchen and found Naomi wrestling a turkey in the sink. She grabbed ahold of Naomi from behind. Naomi turned around and got a good look at her and whooped, and Trixie thought she'd smother her in her bosom. "Look at you! What are you now? Fifteen years old?"

"Seventeen in April!" she said.

"Rafe! Rafe! Look who's come to see us!"

Trixie took his hands and squeezed them hard. Then, before she took off her coat or offered to help Naomi or tried to make small talk with Frank and Edna, she slipped out back and took a walk down the path to the creek. The path had narrowed so much in places that she had to push her way through, and when she reached the creek, she saw no sign of the footbridge, which must have rotted and washed away. The great oak remained, but the boxcar had gone; the railroad company had eventually hauled it away, she supposed. She stood there a good while meditating on the wild beauty of the green laurel, the bare trees, the clear rushing creek, but there was nothing so sad as a place both sad and lovely, and she left it knowing she'd never go there again.

"I don't guess he ever came back?" she asked Naomi when she returned to the house. She warmed her hands over the woodstove.

"Um-hum," Naomi said, cutting her eyes toward Trixie without turning around. "You hadn't been gone two, maybe three weeks when he come. Late one night Miz Edna had gone to Spartanburg. He come by and I filled his belly up good. Said he missed that boat down in Florida and was heading up toward West Virginia. Heard they was hiring again in the coal mines."

"Did he ask about me, Naomi?"

"Um-hum," Naomi said, not looking up. "But I ain't never seen hide nor hair of him since. And ain't likely to again. And you ain't either. So you put that out of your mind."

"I can't, Naomi."

"Yes, you can, too. You just put your mind on something else, like going to see Miss Esther. She's done gone and got herself married!"

"Oh! She never mentioned it in her last letter!"

"To that boy she's been sparkin' off and on all these years. Hurried up and married him before they shipped him off."

Trixie drove to Esther's house and knocked on the door. She and Esther squealed and hugged. Esther held out her hand to show off her ring, and they hugged again. Esther asked Trixie inside, and they had hot tea and tiny, perfect huckleberry tarts that Esther's mother served them. Esther showed Trixie photos of her three-minute wedding held in front of the fireplace right there in her mother's small parlor—Esther, gleaming in a wide-shouldered dress, clutching a spray of winter jasmine, her hair rolled back from her forehead in the style of the day, Teddy White beaming beside her in his sailor suit.

"He still has a baby face!" Trixie said.

They put on coats and hats and walked up the road a half mile or so to where a cute house, covered with gray shingles, peeped out from a dense thicket of laurel halfway up a steep hill—the house where the new couple would start a family when Teddy came home. Esther was sewing curtains for the windows already, she said. She couldn't wait to scour the woodwork, scrub the floors, paint the parlor walls a dusky pink, and put down a wine colored rug. They wanted four children, at least; they'd discussed it already. She even had names picked out.

Although Trixie was the younger of the two of them, she felt old listening to Esther that day; she felt suddenly barren and penniless and, for the first time, just a little envious of Esther. What did she have to look forward to but living with kind, sweet Ollie Pearl among the passionless, childless, clean but dingy walls of her little old house, where everything smelled sickly sweet of rose water, camphor, and pickling spice?

When Frank gave Trixie a real gold bracelet for Christmas, she held her wrist up to the light and watched the gold glisten. "You know, Trixie," Ollie Pearl said, "Frank wouldn't be a bad catch for you."

All the next year Frank sent letters from naval bases in Philadelphia and Charleston and San Diego. Trixie opened them, read them, and folded them up. She felt nothing for Frank, but the attention didn't feel all that bad. A good catch? For somebody, maybe. She wasn't ready to throw out *her* line.

Not that it mattered much in life where you threw out your line or where you set your sights, she was learning. Trixie and Ollie Pearl, back at home in Five Forks, sat in the parlor cracking and shelling pecans for fruitcake, all set to listen to Sammy Kaye's Sunday Serenade on that afternoon of December 7, 1941. "From the NBC news room in New York: President Roosevelt said in a statement today that the Japanese have attacked the Pearl Harbor, Hawaii, from the air. . . ."

It was all the talk on the radio, day and night, all the talk over the fence, by the clothesline, at the store. Lines formed around the enlistment centers in the towns. Everybody's fingers itched to do something, but what? Edna sent Ollie Pearl and Trixie a letter. She was all up in the air about Frank's getting sent to the Pacific. She begged them to please come up for Christmas before he was shipped off, and it seemed like something they could do, so off they went.

So much was the same that last Christmas at Laurel Terrace in 1941, yet much was different. Naomi in the kitchen, but a little more stooped and a little less jolly. Old Jack turning the knob on the radio, not for Jack Benny or the Grand Ole Opry, but to hear what Edward R. Murrow or Eric Sevareid had to say.

Trixie sat by the counter at Mr. Pace's store, not talking girl talk with Esther or watching her polish her nails, but watching her dab at her eyes because her new young husband had gone down with the *Arizona* during the attack on Pearl Harbor. Life went on. Trixie tried to get Esther's mind off the little shingled house on the hill with its dusky pink walls and empty, childless hallways. She tried to get her excited about attending King's Business College in Raleigh, as Trixie planned to do in the spring. They could share a room. Maybe when they graduated they could find a job at the same place, end up in the same typing pool! Trixie made Esther go with her to the theater in town to see *How Green Was My Valley*.

Join the service and make yourself a man was as thick in the air as the cold that Christmas. *Marry a soldier and make yourself a woman* was implied, if never said. If a girl had a soldier boy on the string, she ought to go ahead and marry him so he'd have something to come back to, something to want to survive for when he was neck high in a foxhole with gunshot pocking the mud around his head. Naomi made some good money making cakes for all the hurry-up weddings.

One night Trixie sat in the upstairs room with Ollie Pearl, who had her hair in pin curls and cold cream smeared on her face, just like all the years before. "Now, Trixie," she said when Trixie told her that Frank had written her a letter asking her to marry him, "I'm not going to say you should and I'm not going to say you shouldn't. But I will say you ought to consider it. Very seriously. And I don't mean to sound ugly by saying this, but it's not like you've had other prospects."

"But I don't really know Frank," Trixie said.

"You know him better than I knew your uncle Jarvis or the Colonel. And Mrs. Garfield, over at the church, her daughter married a boy she'd only exchanged letters with and met once. You never really know a man, anyway. You know Frank's family, and that means an awful lot."

"Aren't you supposed to be at least a little in love when you marry somebody? Or compatible or something?"

"Well, Trixie," Ollie Pearl said, wiping the cold cream off her face with a tissue, "love isn't the way they make it look at the moving pictures. It's not always something you fall into. Real love is something you decide to do, then just do, just like you'll take care of your house and the babies when they come. And you know, these days, a girl marries a soldier, she gets upwards of fifty dollars a month! Just for waiting at home and writing him letters! A girl can make good money as a stenographer or typist, but not enough to keep herself up in comfort. And you know when I'm gone you've got my little house to live in, but look around"—she waved her arm across the big room with its heavy moldings, high ceilings, and the potential, according to Esther, to become something close to a mansion—"and see what you might call yours someday!"

She did it for so many reasons, and all of them made sense at the time—for fifty dollars a month; to please Ollie Pearl, without whom she'd be nowhere and have nothing; to show that sometimes the apple did fall far from the tree; for a star in her crown for marrying a soldier and giving him something to survive for; for love of the old house, which was the closest place to a home she'd ever known;

and for the secret hope that someday she might look out the kitchen window and see someone she'd once known for a short while emerge from the path through the laurel—Trixie married Frank in a ten-minute service in the parlor at Laurel Terrace.

Love is something you just do, Ollie Pearl had said. So Trixie just did it. She stood beside Frank in a white suit dress, belted at the waist, with big shoulder pads. Edna had borrowed it from somebody for Trixie to wear, and it hung too loose and too long. She tried to beam like Loretta Young but came off looking twenty years older than she was, twisted and tormented like Joan Crawford. Naomi handed her the silver cake knife with the filigreed handle to cut the white cake. The citrus punch, sipped from morsel-sized glass cups, tasted as bitter to Trixie as the occasion felt. Frank got called back early, and everybody present went to see him leave on the train. He kissed her and she didn't know which was worse, realizing that the man getting on the train was her husband, or the woman left standing beside her at the depot was her mother-in-law.

That Christmas in '41, as in the ones before, they had whatever Naomi could scrape together from all she'd preserved in the fall. They had Naomi's chocolate Yule log and fruitcake. They hung mantels and doorways with green, and a fire flickered in the fireplace in the parlor. Trixie pecked out carols with one finger on the old piano. "I Wonder as I Wander," "O Come, O Come, Emmanuel," "The First Noel." And like always, Ollie Pearl read from the second chapter of Luke. "And it came to pass. . . ," she began, and read the whole Christmas story through. "But Mary kept all these things," she read at the end, "and pondered them in her heart."

Root Hog or Die

On a cold, gray afternoon, the day right after New Year's Day, Trixie received a phone call from Pace's Store, from a softly crying Esther. It was quiet in the store, and in the absence of customers, Esther's mind had traveled the miles to Pearl Harbor, where the thousand or so crewmen of the USS *Arizona*, including Teddy, had perished on December 7. And Esther had just recently learned that most of them, including Teddy, would lie there forever, a thought she was finding unbearable.

Anxious to offer some comfort to Esther, Trixie had slipped on her coat and started out the door, when Edna handed her a list of some things she might as well pick up. Ollie Pearl gave her a twenty-dollar bill. You could buy a lot more than white bread, a dozen eggs, a ten-pound bag of potatoes, and coffee with twenty dollars in those days.

Trixie looked at her, shocked, but Ollie Pearl turned away and said, "Go ahead and buy yourself something with the change." Trixie wondered if this small gesture was meant to ease Ollie Pearl's guilt for coaxing her to marry Frank. "A new handbag or pair of shoes or something."

"You could 'bout get to Norfolk or New Orleans on a twenty-dollar bill," Old Jack said. His comment took root and grew in Trixie's fancy on the winding drive to town.

She found Esther red-eyed but composed. They hugged. They

talked a while. The train arrived, and a soldier came in the door and up to the counter. "Pack of Chesterfields, honey," he told Esther. He picked up a copy of the *Asheville Citizen* and dropped a nickel for it on the counter. UNITED NATIONS DECLARATION SIGNED BY 26 ALLIED COUNTRIES, the headline read. With Esther getting busy at the cash register, Trixie went through the store, quickly picked out what was on the list, and paid Esther. Esther handed her a stick of sassafras candy, some loose change, and several bills that felt pleasingly thick in Trixie's pocket. More passengers trickled in, so Trixie kissed Esther on the cheek and told her they'd talk again later. Trixie went outside to take her groceries to the car.

A little snow swept like dry sand across the road and mixed with the coal dust the steam engines had left behind. Together they looked like salt and pepper caught in the corners between the sidewalk and the street. The air felt colder than ever after she'd left the warmth of the store, so Trixie walked as quickly as she could, with arms full of groceries, to the car. Two soldiers in uniform had stepped off the train and headed for the store. As she put her things in the car, she could see a few stragglers walking off the train behind them.

She had just turned the key in the ignition and situated herself in the driver's seat when somebody moved toward her. A man tapped on the window. He looked large and ghostlike behind it. She slid over to the passenger side, wiped a space clear, then yanked hard at the handle to get the window down. His face was red from the cold, and he hadn't shaved in a day or two. He grinned big and tipped his hat, but they looked at each other a while before either of them spoke.

Trixie's eyes teared up. "Joe!"

"Well, if it ain't the li'l ole pipsqueak! You going to sit there googly-eyed, or move over and let me in?"

She slid back behind the wheel. He threw his duffel bag in the backseat and got in the passenger side. He reached over and turned up the heat. She kept looking at him, stunned. "Is it really you?"

"The one and only! How long's it been now? Six years?"

"I think so," she said. "A little over."

"Look at you! All grown up. A whole foot taller."

"And look at you!" she said. "You're . . . you're a man!"

He laughed. "What'd you expect?"

"You're not half as scrawny."

"They feed us good in Roosevelt's Tree Army," he said. "The CCC, you know. That's what I'm doing, been doing for a while now. Re-enlisted—they run it kind of like the regular army—and I'm heading up to the camp in Mount Mitchell. Still got some work left to do on that road they cut through the mountains up there."

"It sure is good to see you, Joe."

"Good to see you too, kid. Really good. Lot of track gets covered in a few years."

They tried to cover those years in the few minutes they had before the train left again. He'd ridden the rails a while before he joined up at the Civilian Conservation Corps in Buford, Georgia. "I'm still a hobo right in here, though," he said, tapping his chest with his fist. He reached inside his coat, pulled out his train ticket, and flashed it near her face. "Only now when I ride the train, I'm a paying customer! Don't hardly know how to act, either! Feel like a rich man."

"Naomi told me you came by not long after we left. She said you missed the ship down in Florida."

"Yeah and just barely too, just by a day. Missed you, too. She said you all hadn't been gone too many days when I came by. You know, I went by where you lived with that aunt, too, at that little rut in the road, that Five Forks."

"You didn't!"

"Yeah. I'd heard about some work at a fish-packing plant on the coast. I started out that way. Train didn't stop there at Five Forks, but I jumped off on the fly, turned my ankle, limped the rest of the way. Didn't matter. Didn't stop me. Hobbled around town, knocking on this door and that one. Neighbor lady said your aunt got married and moved you off. So you see, kid, I tried. Looks like we were bound to miss each other, like two freight trains passing in the night."

"Don't talk like that, Joe. You'll make me cry."

"Well, anyhow, that job at the fish-packing place was just talk. I rode the rails a while longer after that. Rode hell for leather, seeing what all I could see, drinking up the sights, barely kept alive. Then I joined the camp. Best thing I ever did in my life. Ate good, worked harder than I ever did in my whole life, but got paid for it. Don't know how long it'll last now, though, now that the war's turned everything upside down."

"What all did you do there?"

"Shoot, what all didn't we do? Built roads and bridges, planted trees and kudzu vine all over the roadsides to stop erosion." He stopped and chuckled. He took off his hat and scratched his head. "Yeah, that kudzu vine, it's something else how fast it grows. They told us over and over while we planted it, they said when you stick a sprig in the ground, jump back or it'll reach out and grab you. It'll strangle you to death."

"No, it won't!"

"Sure as the world! One time at the end of the day, we were all piling into the truck to head back to the barracks, when we missed one of the guys in our platoon. 'Where the heck's Harry?' everybody wondered. Well, they looked and looked and finally found him dead underneath a spread of kudzu four feet high and twelve feet wide where it had grown clear over him."

"You're making that up!"

"No I'm not! Did you ever know me to lie to you?"

He looked at her for a long time without saying a thing. "Sure is good to see you again, kid. Guess I ought not to call you that now."

"You can call me that, Joe."

"How about you? What've you been up to?"

She told him that after the Colonel died she and Ollie Pearl moved back to her house at Five Forks; she graduated from high school last year. She planned to take a secretarial course at a business college. She didn't go near the subject of Frank.

"Hey, good for you. It's good to have an education. Wish I had one. Bet you've got the boys beating the door down, too."

"No, not exactly." She wondered when and how she'd tell him about Frank.

"Anybody you crazy about?"

She looked him square in the eyes then. "No." Well, it was the truth. "How about you?"

"Nah. Nothing much."

She didn't say anything for a minute, and he didn't either. The inside of the car was warmer now, and the windows had cleared up. The brakemen hollered back and forth to each other. The two servicemen ambled back toward the train. One of them threw up his hand at Joe, and Joe waved back.

"I got to know those two dogfaces on the way up here," he said. "They're on their way to Fort Mead up in Maryland."

"You going to join up, Joe?"

"You mean the real service? I was all set to, but the officers at the Camp kept telling us all to hold back for a little while, keep at what we're doing. Maybe we'll all get lucky and the war'll be over before summertime."

A few cars started to arrive, men started loading the baggage car, and a handful of people rushed into the depot for tickets.

"Say, kid, remember right before I left, how we used to talk, you and me? We sure were two peas in a pod, weren't we?"

"We sure were."

"You're not working up a cry again, are you?"

"I'll try not to."

"Remember how you thought you wanted to ride the rails with me?"

"Yeah!" They both laughed about it. She thought a minute and then decided to go ahead and tell him about dressing up in Frank's clothes, how she ran as fast as her little legs could carry her down to his camp, where Scoop Shovel had taken it over.

"Good ole Scoop Shovel. Probably died in a ditch somewhere. Reckon that dog's long gone, too. Did you really do that? Dress up like a boy and come running after me?"

"I did!"

"Shoot fire, that took some gall! Hey, remember when you asked me if it would be any different when you were fifteen and I was eighteen?"

"How could I forget?"

"You're what, now?"

"Almost eighteen."

"And I'm twenty-one."

People had started boarding the train. The fireman shoveled coal into the engine. The porter tossed the last bags into the car and wiped his hands.

"Well, looks like I don't have a whole lot of time now, so what I want to say I got to say fast. While we've been sitting here talking, I've been thinking. You know, I've been around and seen a lot. Lot of places, lot of faces. The more I saw, the more your little face kept kind of rising up in my mind."

"Joe—"

He tapped her lips with his finger. "I know. I know a lot of water's gone under the bridge, lot of track covered. I know we were both just kids and didn't know each other but a few days. And I know we don't know each other at all now. But what if, just what if, I wrote you a letter from the camp or wherever I end up. Would that be all right?"

She nodded.

"Maybe you'd write me back?"

"Well, sure I would, Joe."

They got out of the car and he reached in the back and took his duffel bag. They walked toward the train. He swung the bag over one shoulder and took her hand. "And I know I'm just dreamin'," he said, while they walked along toward the train, "but maybe we'll exchange letters for a while, then just maybe when my camp days are up, the war will be over, too, and we could get to know each other. Take it one step at a time, see what happens. Maybe nothing, but maybe something. And, I know I'm really dreamin' now, but I don't have much time, got to say what's on my mind: If it comes down to it, if you decide that maybe you'll have me, well, shoot, with all I learned working at the camps, I can do practically anything to make a living practically anywhere you'd want to go."

"That sounds really good, Joe. Only. . . ."

"Only what?"

The locomotive started its slow, steady *cough, cough, cough* as the engine began to fire up. At the same time, she felt something firing up inside of her. With her hand still in her pocket, she used her thumb to work the ring off her finger. She didn't have a thing with her but the several dollar bills plus change, but she could buy a train ticket with it. Maybe not as far as Norfolk or New Orleans, as Old Jack had said, but she could go quite a ways on it, at least as far as Joe was going, she knew. She didn't need another thing, not a thing in the world that she couldn't get on down the tracks.

He took her by the arm. "Only what?"

"Only . . . why wait? Why can't I just go with you now, Joe? Right now this minute?"

"*What?*"

"Right now!" And she meant it. She'd never felt so fine, never stood so tall as she did right then. The engine fired up. Stragglers rushed out of the depot to board the train.

"Shoot! I don't know if we ought to go about it that way, kid." He shook his head.

"Give me one good reason why not!"

"For one thing, there's no place for a girl at the camp."

"I could stay somewhere outside the camp, get a room with an old lady or something!"

He chuckled. "Have to be an ole granny woman way out in the middle of the woods. And from what I hear, I might get to camp only to find out they're breaking the whole thing up. There's a war on. I get shipped out, where does that leave you? And speaking of old ladies, wouldn't it break her heart, that aunt of yours?"

"I'd write her a letter and explain it all! I'd write it on the train and mail it at the next stop!"

"All aboard!" the conductor yelled out.

She walked fast toward the depot. Joe caught up with her and held on to her elbow. "Where're you going?" he asked.

"I'm going to buy a ticket! I've got the money to buy one right here!" She pulled her hand out of her pocket, the hand with the money in it. She flashed the dollar bills right in his face.

"What's that?" he asked.

Seventeen whole dollars in bills! she almost said, but then she saw him looking at the ground. He stepped a little ways down the road to where the thin gold wedding band had rolled when it fell out of her pocket.

He picked it up out of the dusting of dry snow and coal dust where it had landed. He wiped it clean and brought it back to her, held it out to her in the palm of his hand.

How could she tell him how much it didn't mean to her, how nothing it was? "Okay, I got married—but just a few days ago!"

"To?"

"To Frank."

"*That* Frank?"

She nodded.

"Shoot." He looked at the ground and shuffled his feet. He looked back up at her and shook his head.

"But I didn't want to, not at all."

"Then how come you did?"

"A lot of reasons. Everyone seemed to think I should. . . ."

"He an enlisted man?"

"He's been in the Navy a while. Then the war broke out. We got married before he shipped out to the Pacific."

"That's too bad, kid. That's way too bad. For me, anyhow. For you it might be just the ticket."

A big burst of steam. The blow of the whistle. "All aboard!"

"I'm going with you anyway," she said.

He shook his head. "First off, that Frank, he's flesh and blood; he's got to have a heart. You're a little married woman and all. You run off with me now, you'll have to live it down for the rest of your life."

"I don't care!"

"You know what I'm saying is true, don't you?" He took her by the shoulders, lifted her chin. "Don't you?"

It was true and she knew it, but many times she'd looked back on that moment, knowing if she'd persisted, he might not have turned her away. Why hadn't she?

"Look," he said. "A year from now everything'll look all different. Maybe it'll turn out you did the right thing, after all, marrying Frank. Maybe you'll live right there in that big ole house. I could never give you anything like that. You and Frank, you'll have yourself a passel of kids running around barefoot in the creek." He pulled a handkerchief from his pocket, unfolded it, and wiped at the tears on her face.

"What about you, Joe?"

"Who knows? I might not ever settle down, anyway. Once you got hoboing in your blood, you're bound to wander." He swung his duffel bag over his shoulder and squeezed her hand. "It'll be good," he said. "You and that Frank."

"But Joe?"

"What's that, kid?"

"What if it's not good?" She really, really wanted to know.

He put his finger under her chin. "I don't know. Try to take it one day at a time, that's all I know to tell you. Just keep on moving down the track to the end of the line," he said. "Root hog or die."

Esther

And that's just what Trixie did back in the spring of '42 when she and Ollie Pearl returned home. She took classes at the business school in Raleigh, but only a few, because both Ollie Pearl's and Edna's health started to decline. She did what the posters told her to do, though. LONGING WON'T BRING HIM BACK SOONER. . . , one said, GET A WAR JOB! So she got jobs typing and bookkeeping, and she worked for a while in a factory, making silk threads for parachutes. She thought of a hundred ways to use Spam, grew a big, fine Victory garden, and pickled everything. She sold war bonds, rolled bandages, and put yellow dye in the oleo to make it look like butter. After Edna died, she cut loose a little, though. She kept the dance floor hot down at the River Club on Ollie Pearl's bridge nights until Ollie Pearl found out about it and made her stop because it didn't look good.

With the war finally over, Frank came home. Soldiers and war brides danced in the street. Relief and promise filled the air. The government built apartments for the returning veterans. Trixie and Frank took up residence in one of them until they bought their house. They ran the inn from a distance for a short while with the help of Naomi and Rafe. But with times better, boarders were less genteel, more likely derelict.

Trixie raced through a string of events in her memory, things she'd just as soon forget: the awful day they had to evict Old Jack and find a place for him, Ollie Pearl's death, followed by Rafe's and then Naomi's. And all the while, Frank sowed his wild oats. Of course, she recalled happy moments, too, the birth of her three children, mainly.

And now, all the years later, those same kids—the ones she'd brought into the world, nursed through childhood and their crazy years with simple wisdom and common sense—towered over her and felt entitled to tell her what to do. They'd have conniption fits if they knew she was heading up that steep mountain road in a snowstorm.

Because of the snow, her little trip had taken Trixie a lot longer than she'd thought. What ought to have been a jaunt had turned into a long hard haul. What had started as flurries had turned into snow showers five miles outside of Spindale. Up the mountain the snow showers had become snowfall. Now the headlights burned through the thick fog of snow, and the wipers quivered and scrunched to clear the windshield in half circles she could barely see through. One false move, a slight swerve, a light tap on the brakes, and she could flip over the edge and tumble over and over to the bottom of the gorge! But on she went, root hog or die!

Worry about how she'd get home burned at the back of her mind, but a warm place to sit and rest—even in a rest home!—a visit with Esther, the promise of news about an old friend drove her on. She leaned forward and clamped down on the steering wheel at the ten o'clock and two o'clock positions and inched her way up the mountain.

In Saluda, the little town by the railroad track, tiny white lights rimmed the windows of the shops and the old depot. The whole town looked just like a street in Lou Ann's Snow Village that she put up on a card table every Christmas. As Trixie slowed to turn and drive over the tracks, she could almost see Joe, a boy of fifteen, striding along the street in front of the depot, peddling his strings of chinquapins.

His words echoed and echoed in her mind: *Ten cents for a string, three for a quarter, one for your wife and two for your daughter. . . .*

On she went, but nature had saved the worst part of her drive for last. The white-covered road to Laurel Terrace wound and climbed, twisted and turned; the tail end of her car wagged as she made a tight curve. A harsh light beamed down through the blowing snow over a sign: LAUREL TERRACE: AN ASSISTED LIVING COMMUNITY. She had slowed to turn into the drive, when a snowplow, lights blinking, roared down from the top of the hill, slapping her car with a mix of snow and road grit that darkened the windshield so suddenly and utterly, she felt entombed. "Why, you. . . !" she cried out, slapping the horn, but the truck's taillights had already shrunk to red dots down the road. A moment later, her weary windshield wipers scraped out a fuzzy space she could peer through, if she angled her sight just so. Once she started up the long, winding driveway, she was thankful the plow had beat her there, though she would have liked to have had a word with its driver!

At the top of the hill, not far from where the old inn had once perched, the new Laurel Terrace more or less just squatted, as she had feared. The developer had cut down the top of the hill so that the grounds around the building lay almost flat, too. But they'd left some of the laurel, thankfully. Tiny white lights hung around the front entry; the place wasn't completely cheerless, anyway.

She parked, turned off the headlights and wipers. She let out a long sigh. Finally! She put the scarf around her head and, over it, her hat. When she stepped out of the car, reaching for her pocketbook and the Tupperware cake carrier, her glasses fogged over. She had a time battling the blowing snow to the entrance. Two women in front of her, dressed like Russian peasants and carrying fruit baskets, fought the wind and snow up the concrete ramp.

She stepped up on the covered stoop and tried to shake some snow off herself. She stood there a minute to catch her breath. Why, she felt herself trembling! Trembling with the cold, with excitement.

"Oh, I'm sorry!" she said and hurried to the entryway, where one of the Russian peasants patiently held the door open for her. She stepped inside to heavenly warmth and the scent of cinnamon. She and the two women gave their coats a good shake and hung them in a little alcove just inside.

The people who ran Laurel Terrace had made the lobby appear festive, she had to admit. Sparkling streamers hung in the doorways. A little ceramic Christmas tree sat on the reception desk in the foyer, its colored lights winking. A tall tree strung with flashing bubble lights filled up one corner of the room beyond. Here and there, in chairs and on sofas, sat some of the residents watching or not watching the Grinch steal Christmas from little Cindy Lou Who. Some of them, women and men both, looked fit and glowing like models from *Modern Maturity* magazine. Others looked, well, old. But they all wore thin, stretchy knit caps on their heads. Red ones, for Heaven's sake! Where was she—at a rest home for gnomes? The two women with fruit baskets made a fuss over one of the residents in a foreign language.

In a far corner opposite the tree, a man sat by himself in a wheelchair, gazing out the window, watching the snow come down. The window gave back his face like a mirror, almost. He wore a red knit cap like the others, but his perched high above his ears on the top of his mostly bald head, as if he had started to take it off, poor old thing, then forgot all about it.

A woman came in behind Trixie, took off and hung up her coat. "Whew!" she said. "It's just awful outside!" She plopped down behind the desk, swiveled to face Trixie, and said, "Merry Christmas! How may I help you?"

"Merry Christmas to you, too. I'm Mrs. Goforth, and I'm here to see Mrs. Esther Purvis." Out of the corner of her eye she saw the man in the wheelchair look up her way. Didn't he seem familiar, just the teeniest bit familiar? Like Bing Crosby? Yes, maybe. Or maybe not, she thought, peering through her bifocals to get a good look at him. Maybe she just had Bing on the brain because of the white Christmas and all. But the man kept watching her. He watched her as if from a far greater distance than the other side of the lobby, as if he wasn't quite sure he saw her or not. She felt a feather tickling the back of her neck.

"All right, let me see now." The receptionist stared at the computer screen. "Paley," she said, "Palmer . . . I don't see . . . I can't find. . . ."

So much for those dang computers! Trixie thought.

"Oh there she is! Mrs. Purvis. Room 132. Right down the hall that way and around the corner."

Trixie had already started toward the swinging doors when the woman called out for her to wait.

Goodness, what a scatterbrain!

"I forgot to get you to sign in first, please. It's a rule."

"Well, all right," Trixie said, miffed. People that woman's age didn't understand that when people Trixie's age signed their names they had to do it *right*, so it was a lot of trouble. She had to put down her pocketbook and the cake carrier and wipe down her bifocals with the tail of her sweater and then get the pen situated just so in her fingers.

Trixie could see him out of the corner of her eye, that man in the wheelchair next to the window. Now he fumbled with his own glasses, trying to arrange them on his face. Finally he got them looped around his ears. He stared hard in her direction, until a woman came up and spoke to him. She was a knockout, too, Trixie thought, the kind to turn heads on a cruise ship packed with rich oldsters.

Face-lifted, though. Looked like she'd stormed ninety miles an hour through a wind tunnel.

Trixie flicked her wrist a couple of times and signed her name slowly and with a flourish.

"Thank you, Mrs. Goforth," the receptionist said.

Trixie nodded, picked up her purse and cake carrier, shouldered her way through the swinging doors, and started down the hall. The doors swung shut, trapping her, so she felt, in an eerily quiet maze of long, white tunnels. Pretty pictures—pastures and forests and lily pads floating in still water—lined the walls of the corridor, but it still felt so empty. Well, the hallway *was* empty, which stood to reason; many of the residents would have gone elsewhere on Christmas Eve, the lucky ones anyway. Even Esther.

Trixie stopped dead in her tracks. Why hadn't she thought of that? Esther's daughter might have come to get her already! No, not that old hippie of a daughter of hers, Tilly, the kind who'd rather snowshoe with her mangy dogs than pay attention to her poor old mother. Of course Esther would be there. That receptionist woman, though harried, ought to know who had gone away for the holidays and who had stayed.

Trixie had just rounded the corner into another long hallway when she heard the door from the lobby open and shut with an echo. Then she heard a *whirr . . . click click . . . whirr . . . click click* sound, growing closer and closer, it seemed, then slowing, then stopping. Something about that lone sound in the empty hallways spooked her. She stepped livelier then, almost running right past rooms 130 and 131.

Room 132. Finally! She tapped lightly on the door and went on in, not giving Esther a chance to answer. She shut the door behind her and turned around.

"Esther?" she said, almost out of breath. "Esther?" she said again, looking behind the door to the bathroom. No Esther in the room, but Trixie sensed she'd just left it. She twitched her nose. Was that a whiff of gardenia body spray that smelled so . . . so Esther?

That ugly macrame hanging was not Esther, though. Maybe it was a gift from somebody, maybe that weird daughter of hers, and she didn't want to throw it away. It had a brass pot of philodendron in it. Trixie pinched off the long, leggy parts, then fingered the soil—a touch dry. She found a drinking glass by the sink in the bathroom—rose lipstick print on the rim of it—and gave the plant some water.

Esther had put pictures in pretty frames on every flat surface in her room, pictures of her kids and grandkids, of her second husband, Gus, in his military uniform. Trixie picked up a picture of Esther and Gus standing in front of the *Arizona* Memorial in Hawaii. Gus had been a good man who had taken her to Pearl Harbor to pay respects to her first husband, Teddy, her fallen soldier. Esther looked ever so pretty in that pink and green muumuu, with a lei around her neck and an orchid in her hair.

"Esther! Where are you?" she snapped, stamping her foot. She had a weird impulse to look under the bed, the only place she hadn't checked already. No Esther, but a pair of silky red slippers, lying just under the frame, as if kicked off in a hurry. Of course, she would expect Esther to wear red slippers around Christmastime. Trixie pulled them out and lined them up neatly by the bed. Maybe if Esther hadn't gone home with her daughter, she'd gone down to the café for a bite of something. Was she getting her hair fixed for Christmas Day? Or having a little visit with her man friend? Trixie hooted at that thought! She sat down on the chair by the bed. What a day! She was starting to feel positively silly.

She noticed the Christmas cards that Esther had taped everywhere. Then she noticed the one with all the Christmas seals on it, the one Trixie had sent her. It lay faceup on the nightstand under a gaudy lamp. She clicked on the lamp and picked up the envelope. Why, Esther hadn't even opened it yet! Talk about absentminded! Maybe just the effects of being in love! Right next to it lay Esther's plastic pillbox: "M" for Monday, "T" for Tuesday, and so on, just like the one Trixie had at home. An old woman's rattle; that's what Trixie called it.

She picked up the pillbox and shook it and popped open one of the little compartments to see what Esther was taking. She nodded her approval: estrogen, coated aspirin, calcium, Inderal. (Buck had taken Inderal for his heart. Lots of people took it.) And the all-important fiber pill! Trixie had lately started using the powdered stuff you mixed up in a glass of water. You had to drink it real fast before you gagged, but it worked better than the pills. She'd tell Esther about it when she saw her. She put down the pillbox and picked up a picture in an oval frame that stood on the nightstand beside Kleenex in an English-lavender-patterned box.

The picture featured Esther with her China doll skin, her surprised eyes, her hair just so, as always. The curly perm looked good on Esther. A Mohawk would look good on Esther. She stood in front of a rose garden somewhere, the gardens at the Biltmore Estate it looked like, yes, in the rose garden in front of the big brick and glass conservatory at Biltmore. Come to think of it, in one of her recent letters, Esther had written that a group of the residents planned to go up there on an outing. You could almost mistake Esther for one of the roses, she had such a rosy blush on her face. The blush of love? The man standing with her must be Esther's—what would she call him? Gentleman friend, man friend, partner, significant other, beau?

Lover? Oh mercy! What scenes that brought to mind! She couldn't wait to pick on Esther about it! She tilted her head back to line up her bifocals so she could study the picture close up, to see just how well Esther had done for herself in the man department. He looked all right—bright eyes, broad smile. Teeth looked real. Trixie could tell real teeth a mile off. Awfully long earlobes, though. But didn't he look familiar? What was the matter with her, thinking everybody she laid eyes on she'd seen before? But this man, quite old, leaning on a cane, looked awfully, awfully familiar. . . .

What was that? She heard that spooky *whirr click click* sound coming down the hallway again, coming closer and closer, a little louder, a little louder. Then it stopped. One moment of total silence. A knock at the door! She didn't answer. She just sat there fingering the Christmas pin on her collar. A dull thud against the door! She looked up at the door, her heart aflutter. The door handle went down slowly, slowly, and snapped back up with a jolt! She gasped. The door eased open, slowly, slowly, and in the crack appeared two feet wearing tan bedroom slippers. Attached to the feet were two very white, very unhairy ankles, one showing an ugly scar where the pants leg had slipped up toward the knee.

The door opened wider. The man she'd seen in the lobby! He wheeled himself right on in like he owned the place. And let the door fall shut behind him! Trixie didn't feel at all comfortable being alone in a room behind a closed door with a man to whom she'd never even been introduced, and she had opened her mouth to tell him so when all of a sudden she *knew* she recognized him. They adjusted their glasses to look at each other. Then she looked at the picture, then the man, then the picture again. Then, with her eyes lit up and spread wide, at him again.

"You're right, Mrs. Goforth," he said, nodding briskly. "That's me in that picture. That's me back in August when I still had use of my legs." He wheeled himself a little closer and held out his hand. "I'm Jim Cunningham, Esther's boyfriend!"

Boyfriend? "Oh!" she blurted out. Her hand flew straight to her mouth.

He wheeled himself closer again. He held his mouth straight and solemn, but his eyes twinkled behind his bifocals. He wagged his finger. "If you're hankering for details, though, you're out of luck. I never was one to kiss and tell! And I apologize for not getting here sooner; I had to attend to a private matter in my room. And before that, Jacqueline detained me back in the lobby. She's hardly my type—too eager!—but I hated to be impolite to her. I think she has, as the youngsters put it these days, 'the hots' for me."

Oh! How fresh! Trixie tried to look disapproving, but she had to swallow to keep down a big giggle bubbling up in her like an Alka-Seltzer plopped in water.

"Are you all right, Mrs. Goforth?" he said a moment later, wheeling himself closer in again. "You look like you're about to have a spasm or something."

She thought he was enjoying her agony way too much.

"Is it by any chance my hat that's tickling your funny bone? Should I take it off then?" He reached up and, with a frisky flip of his wrist, plucked the cap off, making what few strands of hair he had stand straight up.

Well, that did it. She really cut loose then. She bent over double, and when she looked up again, he just sat there in that wheelchair and watched her like she was putting on a show he'd paid good money to see. She laughed so hard, she had to catch her sides. Finally she had to remove her glasses and take a Kleenex from the fancy box on the nightstand to wipe her eyes. "Oh! I'm so sorry!" she said, sniveling, trying to get herself together.

"It's all right, Mrs. Goforth. I know you're not laughing at me! You're laughing with me, as they say!"

Well, let him think that if he wants to.

"It's good to laugh," he said. "We all ought to laugh while we can."

"Thank you!" When she blew her nose, it sounded like a demolition. "You see, I really, really needed that."

He nodded slowly. "I thought you might."

"There, Mrs. Goforth," Mr. Cunningham said, patting her hand a few minutes later. "Go on and cry until you get it all out."

And she did. She cried and cried until she'd turned nearly every one of Esther's Kleenexes into wet balls piled up on the nightstand. She cried because just a few minutes after her laughing fit, after a little small talk to cushion the blow to come, Mr. Cunningham told her that Esther had died in her sleep earlier in the week after two days in the hospital. Her heart.

"But why?" she asked.

"Well, now, Mrs. Goforth, that's an age-old question, and even someone as old as I am doesn't have the answer to that."

"I don't mean why did she die, for Heaven's sake! What I mean is, why didn't somebody tell me? Why didn't that woman at the front desk have the decency to tell me before I came back here looking for Esther?"

"Maybe no one had told her yet. She's quite new and she doesn't know most of us. She's been away for a few days and had just got in when you spoke with her. We're terribly understaffed here, too. Perhaps we don't attract the most efficient or the most sensitive people."

"Other than that, what was the reason? So she's been away for a few days, wouldn't you think that somebody would have grabbed her and told her about Esther as soon as she came in the door a while ago?"

"Understand, Mrs. Goforth, that at a place like this, somebody's passing on is not terribly unusual."

"But how about that sorry daughter of Esther's? Why didn't she let me know?"

"I'm sure she planned to, Mrs. Goforth, but I admit Tilly and her siblings are a rather unusual, disorganized bunch. They held the service only the day before yesterday. As you can see, they haven't had either the time or presence of mind to come back and remove her things." He looked around the room. "It can wait a day or two, until after Christmas."

She blotted her nose with a wet Kleenex, sniffled, and put her hand out and touched Esther's plastic pillbox on the nightstand. She picked it up and rattled it again. "Yes, I guess you're right. She doesn't need any of these things, now."

Trixie looked at the white hairs trailing from Esther's hair pick that lay on the dresser. The narrow closet stood ajar, and in it she could see the edge of Esther's mauve London Fog all-weather coat. A piece of pink plastic wrap spilled out of one pocket. Esther probably carried it with her to cover her hair if it rained. Esther always protected her hair from the rain. She liked to be color coordinated at all times, too.

"What did she wear?" Trixie asked. "At the service?"

"The royal blue dress she wore at her granddaughter's wedding. And the matching blue mesh hat. White gloves. She looked lovely."

Mr. Cunningham picked up the picture in the oval frame and looked at it a while without saying anything. He had come to Laurel Terrace in August, he said after a while. He and Esther had met on the home's little outing to Carl Sandburg's house, but they'd become better acquainted on the bus trip to Biltmore. "I became wheelchair-bound shortly after this picture was made," he said. "But we didn't let that hinder us, not in the least. We looked forward to going back to the gardens at Biltmore in the spring. Esther wanted to see the tulips. She thought a great deal of you, Mrs. Goforth. She spoke of you often."

They were silent for a while.

"Let's go elsewhere, why don't we?" he said. "It won't do for us to stay here."

"It's as if she just walked out of the room," Trixie said before they closed the door behind them.

"I'm inclined to believe, Mrs. Goforth—or perhaps I choose to believe—that that is, quite simply, what she did."

They passed two rooms with closed doors, then a room with the door half opened. She felt like if she held the door back a little farther with her hand she might see Esther standing there, having stepped into the other room to borrow some hairpins from her neighbor.

"Suppose the two of us have a cup of hot apple cider in the lobby," Mr. Cunningham said. "Then, if you can spare the time, I'd appreciate it if you'd help me with a little project I've begun. I promise it won't take long."

Mementos

Trixie could spare the time. She had all the time in the world. That was the problem. To think how she'd fought the very idea of the Methodist Home, and here she was stuck on Christmas Eve at a rest home, of all places, trapped in a snowstorm with a bunch of geriatric elves. She'd either have to call the kids to come get her or stay the night. She'd have to call the kids to tell them what she'd done, like she'd soiled her pants or something! Was there no end to the indignities of old age? And worse, she'd have to disrupt their Christmas. But she couldn't stay here all night, and even if she did, she couldn't let them all get to her house the next day and find her gone, could she? All the ingredients for a major uproar!

When she and Mr. Cunningham returned to the lobby, she became all flustered and placed a call to Terry Wayne and let the phone ring and ring until she remembered that it was Christmas Eve, after all, and all of the kids would be with their in-laws. Terry Wayne would be at Phyllis's parents' house. They'd done Christmas that way for years.

Lucky for her, when the kids had issued her those dog tags, they'd also filled out a little book of phone numbers for her to use, in case she got lost or confused and couldn't reach either of them. "We wrote everybody's number in it but the President's!" Terry Wayne had bragged when he tucked it into the little zipper pouch in her pocketbook. Sure enough, he did. All her children's home numbers and cell phone numbers and their children's numbers, work numbers, even in-law numbers.

She called the number for Phyllis's parents. The phone rang and rang. Her hand trembled and she held the phone so hard against her ear, it hurt. Finally somebody picked up the phone. She heard talking in the background and Johnny Mathis singing, *Chestnuts roasting on an open fire. . . .* Her daughter-in-law's family were just the kind to listen to Johnny Mathis, the kind to have split-pea soup on Christmas Day so everybody wouldn't get so stuffed. Heaven forbid she ever had to spend Christmas at that house. *Jack Frost nipping at your nose. . . .*

Her little great-grandson Trevor answered, and she told him to get his grandpa to the phone and to hurry.

"What's wrong, Mama?" Terry Wayne asked when he came to the phone.

"Terry Wayne, I'm. . . ."

Tiny tots with their eyes all aglow will find it hard to sleep tonight. . . .

"You're *where,* Mama?"

She told him again, then said, "Terry Wayne, have somebody turn down that infernal caterwauling so you can hear me talk!"

"I can hear you fine, Mama! I just can't believe what you're telling me! You did *what?*"

"I know, Terry Wayne. I know it was a stupid thing to drive by myself up the mountain to a nursing home in a snowstorm on Christmas Eve. You don't have to tell me that."

A long silence.

"*Why*, Mama, *why?*" he finally said. She could see Terry Wayne's face twitch, his shoulders jerk, his arms wave around like he'd jumped out of a plane without a parachute.

"Spare me all the *where, what, when,* and *why!*" she barked. "I want you to come and get me! Or on second thought, leave me up here. It'll save you all a trip to the Methodist Home!"

As soon as she hung up the phone, she wished she hadn't called at all. Before long her whole family, her daughter-in-law's family, and then all of Rutherford and Polk counties would be abuzz with Trixie Goforth's folly.

And she hated the thought of his trying to drive up the mountain in that mess outside. What if he had a wreck? Oh mercy! She picked up the phone to call him back and tell him not to come. But he'd come anyway. Besides, what in the world would she do with herself at this loony bin place all the livelong night? She watched the red-capped residents wandering into the lobby from hallways or watching the TV. Maybe she could ignore them, as long as they stayed in their place and didn't cut loose square dancing or something. She guessed the people who ran this place would have to put her up for the night. But where? Of course, Esther's room was empty, but she just couldn't stay there. Oh, what an awful thought.

"Christmas a humbug, uncle?" asked Scrooge's nephew on the TV. "You don't mean that, I am sure!"

"I do," said Scrooge. "Merry Christmas! What right have you to be merry? What reason have you to be merry?"

All the time she had talked on the phone to Terry Wayne, Mr. Cunningham had sat a few feet away. On a table next to him sat a huge, round tray of little paper cups of apple cider. Beside the cups sat a plate of red-nosed reindeer cookies and the Tupperware carrier with Trixie's fruitcake in it. She'd seen him sipping one of the cups of cider, pretending to hear Scrooge and his nephew argue, not Trixie and her son.

Trixie sat down on the edge of a sofa near his wheelchair. He smiled big and offered her some cider.

"I'm just stuck here," she said, taking the little cup. She upturned the cup and knocked back the cider with one swallow. She half wished it had been a shot of whiskey.

"There are worse places, Mrs. Goforth. Look around you. See how festive the staff here at Laurel Terrace has made the lobby? Wasn't it a splendid idea they had for us all to wear these red caps? They're showing these delightful Christmas films into the night, and in a little while one of our volunteers is scheduled to bring her electronic keyboard and lead us in singing carols. She plays 'God Rest Ye Merry, Gentlemen' with such spirit!" He danced his fingers around in the air, mimicking someone playing a piano. "Throws in a little improvisation now and again!"

She looked at him over her bifocals. "They don't let you out of here much, do they?"

"Ha! Ha ha ha!" He slapped his knees and guffawed until several of the others turned their heads and stared. He stuck his knuckles into his mouth to restrain himself but kept whimpering a while afterward.

"Don't be cross, uncle!" said Scrooge's nephew.

"What else can I be," growled Scrooge, "when I live in such a world of fools as this? Merry Christmas!"

Trixie looked around at all the red caps. She doubted if half of the people wearing them could carry a tune in a bucket. She knew she couldn't.

"You'll join us in our sing-along, won't you?" he asked her, when he recovered.

"Oh! Mr. Cunningham, please!" She laid her head in her hands.

For want of anything better to do, to ease her nerves, and because she couldn't stand the thought of good food going to waste, Trixie walked around and offered everybody a slice of fruitcake. Most of the inmates took it, and some of them actually ate it, too. Mr. Cunningham picked at the crumbs on the cake plate and slipped them into his mouth, his eyes darting toward a nurse handing another resident a pill and a cup of water.

"Mr. Cunningham, why don't you just go ahead and eat this last piece of fruitcake instead of picking at the crumbs?" Trixie asked him, picking up the plate and sticking it right under his nose.

The nurse slid her eyes toward him. "I have my eye on you, Mr. C!" she said. "You done had enough of that sweet cider, too."

"That's why," he said, leaning toward Trixie, whispering behind his hand, pointing to the nurse. "That's Latisha. I've got a touch of diabetes, you see, and she loves to plague me about it.

"Would you be a dear, Latisha?" he asked the nurse. "Do you know that box of pictures and mementos in the shelf above my closet?"

"You mean that box of junk?"

"If you pass my room while you're making your rounds, would you mind bringing it to the dayroom?"

She put her hand on her hip and frowned and rolled her eyes.

"Come now, Latisha. Humor an old man."

"You behave, I might," Latisha said, sashaying out of the room.

"Come along to the dayroom, Mrs. Goforth. I'd like you to help me with something. And wrap up that fruitcake. I might nibble on it when Latisha's not looking!"

"Oh, no you won't," Trixie said. "I'll keep an eye on you myself." But she knew if she left it there, it might go to waste, so she put it back into the Tupperware and took it with her. She walked beside him, the wheelchair whirring and clicking as Mr. Cunningham rode down the hallway.

"I'm glad I met you today, Mrs. Goforth, even though neither one of us would have chosen the circumstances. I get lonely here, as you may suspect. Make no mistake about it, my eyes have dimmed but not my appreciation for the company of fine-looking women."

"Mr. Cunningham! Talking like that at our age! And so soon after Esther!"

"We shall both be watching the cracks in our eyelids soon enough, Mrs. Goforth." He reached out and grabbed a fistful of air. "At our age we must seize the moment!"

They entered the dayroom, which had one wall made of windows, all frosted over from the snowy cold outside. Trixie started to walk over and rub a place clear so she could look out, but she wanted to sit down again. What a day! All that driving uphill against the snow, her shoulders sore from leaning over at the steering wheel, hearing about Esther, fighting with her son on the phone. Well, one thing had come out of this uproar. She'd finally met Esther's gentleman friend. And wasn't he a pistol?

Like a real estate agent showing a house, he waved his arm around. "As you can see," he said, "we have a piano in this room, a card table, several conversation areas, but no radio." She knew he meant television. "The dayroom is meant to be a place for pleasant conversation or contemplation."

She looked around the empty room. "Looks like most people would rather watch TV in the lobby than converse or contemplate in here," she observed. Somebody had strung some garland around a big chalkboard and across the piano. Beside a sofa and some chairs sat an aluminum Christmas tree on a side table. Beside it, on the floor, a small disk turned round and round, throwing different colored lights onto the shiny aluminum branches. Mr. Cunningham settled beside it, and Trixie took a seat not far from him.

When Latisha came and brought the box, Mr. Cunningham told Trixie to pull her chair up closer to his so they could look through it together. He seemed awfully excited about it. Latisha put it down on his lap and took off the lid for him.

The box looked full, positively full of junk of all kinds. Trixie liked her own junk, but someone else's, well. . . .

"I don't know why you think your friend'll want to look at all your stuff!" Latisha said.

"You are right about that, Latisha." He looked at Trixie and winked hard. "But it will help Mrs. Goforth and me pass some time."

"Um-hum. He can talk a blue streak, now," Latisha warned Trixie. "All the strength went out his legs and in his mouth."

And so the snow fell outside as the day was winding down. Far away in the lobby somebody played the keyboard. It sounded like a xylophone. Faint little scraps of Christmas carols ("Angels We Have Heard on High," that awful "Rudolph") floated down the long hallways. Trixie pictured Latisha and some helpers trying to corral all the residents in the lobby, trying to get them all in tune to sing that silly red-nosed reindeer song, and having a pretty rough time of it. There in the dayroom, the color wheel turned around and around, coloring the silver branches of the aluminum tree, and Trixie watched Mr. Cunningham's face go red, then green, then gold, then blue as they sat side by side and started to look at his mementos of days gone by.

"Humor me for just a few moments, Mrs. Goforth." He spoke low, even though no one but the two of them was in the room. "When I gave up my home and moved to Laurel Terrace, I had to get rid of a great many things. I brought little with me except a few clothes and this box. Now that Esther has gone, I've found I have the urge to divest myself of everything, like a marathon runner who is making ready to sprint ahead and wants nothing to weigh him down. In the coming weeks, I plan to give away everything in this box. Esther was well aware of my intentions, which is why she wrote to you urging you to come here. You can't imagine how happy it made me to see you walk in the lobby today, because I have a little something here that might interest you, if I can only find it." He rooted through the piles of cards and pictures.

"What is it?" He had *her* whispering, for Heaven's sake!

"Patience, patience! All things worthwhile are worth waiting for."

But while he rummaged through the mess, he insisted on showing her pictures of family members and people she couldn't possibly know, and she knew she could hardly refuse to look. There was his favorite nephew and his family who lived in Seattle. His nephew worked for Boeing, he said.

"What a pity they live so far away," she said. "Did you think about getting into a home there?"

"Oh, I have plenty of other relatives here. This is where I grew up, the place I call home. Besides," he said, showing her an old postcard of Devils Tower National Monument in Wyoming, "I don't really care that much for the scenery out west, which I saw so much of in my youth. Breathtaking as it is, it's too severe for everyday living. Living there would be like living every day in the arms of a flamboyant flamenco dancer. Our Blue Ridge Mountains, on the other hand," he said, showing her another old postcard, one of Blowing Rock, "are like a lovely modest woman who delights, but doesn't overpower, the senses.

"Like my dear late wife, Thelma." He pulled from the pile a picture of his wife. He looked at it a long time without saying a word.

Trixie laid her hand on his arm. "How long has it been since she died, Mr. Cunningham?"

"Twenty-two years. We had a splendid marriage, though no children." He cleared his throat, put the picture aside, then started picking through the rest of the things, claiming he was looking for something in particular, but stopping and showing her things along the way.

He showed her a newspaper clipping gone yellow and starting to crumble inside a plastic sleeve. She strained her eyes through her bifocals and finally made out a man cradling what looked like a five-foot-long zucchini. MAN GROWS MYSTERY VEGETABLE! the headline read.

"Ah, yes, that's me," he said. "It just sprang up in our garden some years back."

Mr. Cunningham, I'm really not that interested in your zucchini! she wanted to scream, but then she thought it would sound ugly.

"A team of agricultural experts from North Carolina State University examined it," he said, "but they never identified it. It relieved me, frankly. I love a mystery to remain a mystery, don't you, Mrs. Goforth?"

She looked up from the picture to his twinkling, teasing eyes. "Not always," she said. Especially the little mystery about what he wanted to show her. If he ever got around to it.

"Why don't you describe what it is you're looking for, Mr. Cunningham? Maybe then I can help you find it."

"A small pouch, hardly bigger than the palm of your hand, in some kind of faded fabric, and an old envelope, as well. But please, would you mind not calling me Mr. Cunningham? Would you mind calling me Jim?"

"All right, Jim," she said, taking her hands out of the box and scooting back from him just a little. She didn't volunteer to have him call her by her first name, though. A woman ought not to come across too familiar too soon.

"Oh, here's our class picture at the old Saluda School!" He held a photograph of a small group of students sitting on the steep flight of steps at the school. "Esther was in the class behind me, did you know that?"

"You knew Esther way back then?"

"I knew *of* Esther, would be more accurate. I left home at an early age, you see. But I admired her from afar, in the tradition of courtly love. In my mind," he went on, "it is nothing short of a miracle that after many years lived, many miles traveled, Esther and I both arrived like homing pigeons right here in Saluda. And at Laurel Terrace! Esther told me that you and the old place share some history."

He prodded Trixie to talk about it, and she told him how she came with Ollie Pearl on Christmas, how that led to her marrying Frank at the onset of the war. It surprised her to find herself confessing to that man—a stranger—that she'd married her husband and the father of her children mainly because of the war.

"Forgive yourself, Mrs. Goforth. Everyone from our generation became who they are largely because of the war. Our times decide our paths as much as anything, whether we like it or not, whether we want to believe it or not."

"You know, Jim, I believe you're right."

"Oh, yes! Take me, for an example. I fought alcoholism for a goodly part of my life. Alcohol was the only way I found comfort after being held as a POW for seven months. I was a machine gunner in the infantry and was captured during the famous Battle of the Bulge, you know."

"Were you for a fact?"

"Indeed." He came across a tiny photograph, four inches square, of himself as a young man in his military uniform. The picture, in sepia tones, had faded. "Here I was, just after I enlisted, before my capture, after which time I was forced to eat rats, cats, snakes, and bugs to stay alive."

"Oh, how awful!" she said.

"I'm quite squeamish about what I eat today, all these years later. Ask the cafeteria staff. That's why I'm so partial to sweets. Of course,

I'd known hard times before, as did most of us who came up in the Depression. Like many boys of our generation, I rode the rails for a few years, looking to make an honest dollar. Racked up quite a few miles, quite a few experiences, educated myself somewhat, exercised my wits. After crisscrossing the country, seeing nearly every big city, small town, and whistle-stop along the way, I came back here. And I can attest that there truly is no place like home."

She had only half listened to him as she rummaged through the mess, desperate to help him find the mystery object. She found a small disk and held it in the palm of her hand.

"Those are wooden nickels the hoboes used to carve," he said. "We'd carve them in our spare time and trade them for goods. You've no doubt heard the saying 'Don't take any wooden nickels'?"

She nodded.

"That was good advice way back when. What is it, Mrs. Goforth?"

"My goodness!" she said, putting her fingers on her throat, where her heart had just leapt. "You were a hobo, Mr. Cunningham?"

"Indeed I was, Mrs. Goforth. But please call me Jim—James Ray Cunningham is my full name—or, as I was called in those days, J. B., for Jungle Buzzard." He laughed. "That was my moniker. Nearly all of us had one, you know."

"J. B.?" she asked again. "*You're* Jungle Buzzard?"

His eyes twinkled. His smile spread wide across his face. He pulled up his pants leg and showed her the scar on his ankle. "My trademark," he said, "courtesy of Texas Slim and his crowbar, some seventy years ago."

Epiphany

"And now, Mrs. Goforth, I think I see the object I've been looking for, down near the bottom."

She watched him, less interested now in what he had to show her, more interested in the fact that here sat Jungle Buzzard not two feet away. *News of an old friend,* Esther had said. "Mr. Cunningham—"

"J. B.!" He wagged his finger.

"J. B., I've got so much I want to ask you now."

"And I shall answer every question you have, Mrs. Goforth. If I can."

"Not till you take your pill now, Mr. C." There stood Latisha. She might have come right out of the wall.

"Must I, Latisha?"

"No, you don't have to take it, if you'd rather start taking them insulin shots."

"Oh, but that pill makes me so drowsy, and as you can see, I have a very special guest."

Latisha put her hands on her hips. "I've told you and told you that there ain't a thing in the world in that pill to put you to sleep," she said. "I keep telling you that's all in your head. You always nod off this time of day, no matter what, and you'll nod off even quicker this evening because you done wore yourself out talking. Probably be out like a light in ten minutes."

Trixie could see that was true. Over the past few minutes, his sparkling eyes had started to dim. He took the pill. Trixie prayed he'd stay awake long enough for her to ask him the many questions springing up in her mind.

"One of these days, Latisha, I'm going to throw you over my knees and give that big bottom of yours a good spanking!"

She let out a whoop and strutted out the door.

"As you can see," J. B. said when Latisha left the room, "we have many hours here to talk over old times. So we talked, Esther and I, about lost times and lost loves. Our own, and those of others. In the course of one of our conversations, a name came up that Esther assured me you would remember."

Trixie's heart hammered in her chest, and she could feel her eyes watching him like a dog hungry for a scrap from the table.

"Pistol Pete," he said, his voice ragged now. He paused a little bit longer between his sentences. He closed his eyes, remembering. "Alabama Broom, Father Todd, Captain Jack, Mad Dog. They all came under my tutelage during my years as resident jungle buzzard up and down the East Coast, and I like to think they survived because of it. You see, some of the 'boes gave me the name Jungle Buzzard in jest. A true jungle buzzard lingers at hobo jungles and leeches off the others. I tended to linger as well, but to offer guidance to the newer ones.

"What a resourceful lot we all were back then. Forced onto the rails looking for a way to make an honest dollar, most of us ended up doing headstands in trash cans, living like common curs. But making a fine job of it, each of us with a style all his own. And most of my 'boes went on to make good in various trades and professions. The poet Carl Sandburg was a hobo, you know, as was television star Art Linkletter, though I don't claim to have tutored the likes of them. But Charmin' Harmon, Flatcar Farley, and Slow Freight Bill all bear the mark of this old Jungle Buzzard.

"And then there was Joe," he said. "Hobo Joe. Simple, unpretentious, unimaginative name. Not the fastest to catch out a freight, always hesitant to put the arm out on a stranger—that is, in hobo lingo, to beg. And yet, Joe was somehow every man, every boy. Every 'bo. Of many, one."

I'm kinda like a mutt myself, she recalled Hobo Joe had said one time. *Little bit of this, little bit of that. Nothing that stands out in particular. Ain't got no flags to wave.*

"So here it is, Mrs. Goforth. When I showed it to Esther, she thought you ought to have it. And I couldn't agree more." From near the bottom of the box he took out a grayish pouch.

At first glance she thought of the pouch she'd made for Joe so long ago—had he kept it all those years?—but this one was made out of some velvety material, very old, and moth-eaten.

J. B. laid it in her hands. It was heavy for its size. A small picture in a heavy frame, she guessed, she hoped. How she hoped! Oh, the times she'd closed her eyes and tried to really remember what he'd looked like. Nothing in the world would please her more. She pulled open the little drawstring of the pouch.

"I last saw Joe when I stopped by here the Christmas of '35," J. B. said. "We slapped each other on the back and spoke briefly. I passed on some news I'd learned about work on a tanker leaving from Tampa. I enlisted shortly after the war began. In '42 I was dispatched to Fort Benning, and somehow or another, through the hobo grapevine, I heard Joe had enlisted after his stint with the CCC. The government more or less dissolved the camps soon after the war began, keeping on some men to fight wildfires or to work at other defense projects. Many of the men, including Joe, enlisted then.

"I heard nothing more from or about him until 1955 at my company's ten-year reunion. In many ways, for veterans, the past is far more real than the present. The war experiences were so intense, the friendships so deep. You wanted to hear what became of this one, that one. Memories remained quite sharp then; many of us who bore no battle scars were still the walking wounded. We'd all lost comrades, friends. Many had foxhole stories to tell.

"And one who had such a story—I can see his face, but his name escapes me now—was in Joe's company somewhere in western Germany. When their company advanced toward the enemy lines, a bullet hit Joe in the chest, but remarkably it didn't penetrate. Another bullet grazed him in the shoulder. He was hospitalized for those injuries, and in a short time he recovered."

Trixie had taken out the little treasure and laid it in the palm of her hand. It was a pendant suspended from a purple and white ribbon. It had a cameo of George Washington in the deep purple middle and a tiny shield of two stripes and three stars in the little dip in the heart at the top. Gold rimmed the edges.

"So he did recover?"

"Indeed he did. As I'm sure you know, the Purple Heart is given to soldiers who have been wounded, as well as to those who have died in the line of duty."

She turned it over. On the back, above a raised bronze heart, it said, FOR MILITARY MERIT / JOSEPH STANLEY CALDWELL.

An old friend, Esther had said. *An old, old friend.*

"So, by rights he would have received two medals. What became of the first one we can't know, and it's of no consequence now. Unfortunately, at that point in the war it was common to put infantrymen right back on the front line." J. B. reached into the box and took out an aged brown envelope and laid it on the table. "According to the War Department letter—you'll find it inside the envelope there—his unit was engaged in heavy fighting in the vicinity of

Obermehlen, Germany, when Joe was struck by automatic weapons fire. He died instantly.

"February 8, 1945. It's one of the few dates I remember well and for a good reason. It was three months to the day before the allied forces triumphed in Europe. We all talked about it, how Joe's death on that date was no more tragic than the hundreds of thousands of others, but that the allies were so close, so close to victory when it happened, just three months! It made us feel as if he almost made it."

J. B. was quiet for a while, and then he went on. "Of course, some died a month before, a week before—even the last day of the war. It is strange but true that there are, in wars, in all of life, degrees of senselessness."

She held the Purple Heart up to the light. Its purple center seemed to glow from deep inside. "How did you get this?" she whispered.

"From Joe's stepfather. Following Joe's mother's death, his stepfather found a letter he'd written home, mentioning me, by my given name. My surname was all the address needed back then in such a small town. A package arrived at the post office addressed simply: "J. B. Cunningham. Saluda, N.C." I did get it, as you see. In that envelope you'll find not only the letter from the War Department, but a bonus—a few letters Joe wrote home."

"Oh!"

"Yes. He'd reestablished contact with his mother before the war, and his letters were urgent and surprisingly personal, as if he was in a hurry to document his every thought and feeling, as if to make up for lost time, or, perhaps, as if he knew what lay ahead. You'll find my name mentioned a time or two"—he winked at her—"as well as the name of someone else who evidently lingered on in his memory."

J. B. watched surprise, then delight, dawn on Trixie's face. He nodded slowly. "Yes."

She touched the envelope, then, eyes closed, tapped it gently, as if telling it to wait. She held the medal in her hand and looked at it for a long, long time. Who would she pass it on to, this little symbol of valor? She could see her children going through her things not too far in the future. "What do we do with this?" Lou Ann would wonder aloud, and Terry Wayne and Thomas would shake their heads. Where would it end up, the Purple Heart of a man whose name her children had not heard, whom she had barely known but had never forgotten? Gently, very gently, she put it back inside the little cloth bag and, along with the faded brown envelope, put it into her purse for safekeeping.

She stood up and walked over to a window and ran her hand over a section of it to remove the condensation. On the mountain across the way, a tiny house she hadn't seen before was now aglow with multicolored lights strung along its roofline. It glittered like her tiny jewel pin against her collar. Not far outside the window, near the corner of the building, near the place where the woodshed once stood, she could see the spruce tree, a true giant now, weighted down with snow.

She watched the snow fall for a while. She was still watching it when J. B. started talking again. "But," he said, as if he'd just paused for a few seconds since his last words, "all of that was then, and this is now. That's the thing we must remember in the days we have left, you and I. Seize the moment! Many years ago, as a prisoner of war, I was in a foreign land lying down in cold mud, all alone. But now I'm sitting in my own country, in a warm room, safe from the elements, talking to a lovely, delightful woman, whose company I might seek out if given the slightest encouragement."

She sat down beside him again and he took her hand. "If I could only tell you how grateful I am for everything right now," he went on. "For the decades of life I've been granted, though I'm no more deserving of it than Joe, of any of those boys. I'm so grateful for what I have right this minute. And as if all the bounty of the moment wasn't enough, tomorrow is Christmas Day! Do you know how I'm going to spend Christmas Day, Mrs. Goforth?"

"I'd love it if you'd tell me."

"Well," he began, "the men of the Saluda Presbyterian Church are coming over to make breakfast for us. For all of us here! Then my niece June will come here to get me, and I'll go with her to visit her family in Tuxedo. Such food she'll have! She's a splendid cook, that June. But tomorrow cannot possibly be half as sweet as my anticipation of it right now. Right this moment.

"And this moment is all in the world that matters to me. You see, then I was eating rats and snakes and grass, but now I am eating—or I should say, just a moment ago I finished eating—a piece of fruitcake that was all the more delicious because I knew it was the very last slice."

She watched as he pressed his fingers into the last of the crumbs and put them on his tongue. "Oh! Look what you've done!" she said.

A minute or so later, Latisha poked her head in and asked him if he was ready to be taken to bed for the night. "Mr. Cunningham, I see you grinning like the Cheshire cat!" She glanced down at the empty cake plate. "And I see what you done!" She clicked on a lamp on a table in the corner. "It's okay by me," she fussed. "It's your blood sugar, not mine. I'm done with you. You go into a coma, don't come crying to me!

"Oh, Mrs. Goforth, your son called a few minutes ago and said he and your daughter were at the bottom of the mountain. Had to stop and put chains on his tires. They'll be up after you soon as they can. I reckon you want to stay up a while, Mr. C."

"Just a few minutes more, Latisha."

"Ain't no use me telling you what to do," she said before she left.

He looked so tired all of a sudden, as if he could nod off any minute. Trixie knew once Latisha took him to his room, she'd likely never see him again. She wouldn't come back to this place. She had much business to attend to after the first of the year.

"Mr. Cunningham—J. B.—there's no way in the world I can tell you what this has done for me. All these years, I've never forgotten about Joe, and I've never been able to tell a soul about it, except Esther."

"I understand. The most fragmentary memories of people you barely knew can sometimes be the most precious."

"Yes! But why is that?" She put her hand on his arm. "I'd really like to know."

"I don't know the answer." He talked very slowly now. She thought she really ought not to encourage him to keep talking. "Maybe it's because when you've known someone only a short time, they don't have time to disappoint or to cause pain?"

"Yes," she said. "Maybe. . . ."

"That's only a theory, of course, and if there is anything to it, I don't believe it applies to our Joe. I truly believe he was one in whom there was no guile. Don't you?"

"Yes, I do. I really do."

"I've heard it said that being remembered so highly is compensation, pitiful though it is, for those who have had to die young. They become legends in our minds. They live on in a way those of us who live out our lifetimes can never do." He reached for her hand and she let him take it. "I've so enjoyed talking to you, Mrs. Goforth."

"And I, you, Mr. Cunningham."

He raised a finger. "J. B.!" He watched her, his lips stretched straight and solemn across his face, his eyes tired but all a-twinkle again. "So," he said, "what next?"

"Why, whatever do you mean?"

"Shall we exchange phone numbers at least? We could get together after the first of the year."

"Oh!" She fingered the pin on her collar and looked away. How tempting to spend time with someone who had known Joe longer and better than she had! But it would be all about Joe. It wouldn't be fair.

"I'm not suggesting any . . . impropriety. We might just share a meal in the cafeteria, a game of Bingo."

"Oh! Go on!"

"And why not?" he asked. "Is there someone else?"

She tapped his arm. "Oh! Listen to you!"

In a short while the light outside dimmed, and the windows looked like big squares of murky, milky white. Nightfall. She looked over to remark about it, but his head had slumped over to the side, and the red knit cap clung to it by a few strands of hair. Latisha came in to wheel him back to his room. When she turned the wheelchair around, his cap slid off. Trixie reached down and picked it up and eased it over his head, pulling it down over his ears, before Latisha wheeled him out. The clicking sound the wheelchair made died away, and a door eased shut far away down a long corridor.

Trixie sat down sideways on the piano bench and tapped out "Silent Night" with one finger, missing some of the notes, and tapering off not long into it. She heard singing. It came from the lobby but sounded far, far away. *A thrill of hope, the weary world rejoices!* Andy Williams singing. They must be watching an Andy Williams Christmas special on TV, she decided. Nobody could sing "O Holy Night" like Andy.

Just then she heard a light tapping at the windows. A spray of sleet? *Oh no, please don't let it sleet with my kids out driving the mountain roads!* The only thing worse would be freezing rain. Then it came again, a tapping at one of the windows, harder this time. She walked over and looked out.

The windows had fogged over again. All the white outside seemed to be pressing to get in. She wiped a patch clear as best she could. It was the view from Naomi's kitchen, from a slightly different angle. She could not see sleet, but then, because of the near darkness, how could she? The snowfall had all but stopped, too, best she could tell. The spruce tree, which had stood five times taller than Rafe, now disappeared into the sky, and its branches, weighted down with snow, hung way out beyond the trunk. The lowest branches cast a deep shade over the spread of dark nettles below. The place where the path through the laurel had begun looked all grown over now. The big twisty branches and small green leaves hung thick with snow. The fallen snow rolled out in smooth waves over the hilly yard and in between the trees. Smooth and undisturbed. Almost. Almost.

She felt a hand on her shoulder. She jumped ever so slightly but didn't turn around. She adjusted her glasses and kept her eyes trained on the fallen snow and the shadows cast by the big spruce.

"Mama?"

"Terry Wayne?" she asked, but she still didn't turn around.

"Yeah, Mama. It's me. Lou Ann's here, too. She's getting your car warmed up and scraping the windshield." He put both hands squarely on her shoulders. "It's a pretty sight out there, isn't it?"

"Um-hum. I'm seeing if there's some sleet coming down. I thought sure I heard it sleeting a minute ago."

"It's not sleeting. It's hardly even snowing now. And what are you smiling at so funny? You see something I don't?" He squeezed her shoulders. "Mama?

"Come on, then," he said. He turned her around to face him. "You ready to go?"

She turned to look out one more time, nodded, then walked over to get her pocketbook.

"What's that?" he asked, speaking of the brown envelope sticking up out of it.

"A gift."

"Who from?"

She didn't answer. Oh, for a blessed hour or two at home alone, in her recliner, in her warmest robe, with a steaming cup of tea and squeaky clean bifocals!

"Terry Wayne, I don't blame you if you're mad," she said as they walked out of the dayroom and down the long hallway. I feel just awful I've gone and caused a big mess right here at Christmas."

He put a big strong arm around her. She was lucky to have a son. Two fine sons, a fine daughter, all of those grandchildren and great-grandchildren, all of them alive, all of them well.

"It's okay, Mama," he said. "There's tomorrow yet. And we'll have plenty of other Christmas Eves."

She guessed she'd let him believe that. "Terry Wayne, you know why I did what I did, don't you? I drove up here to see Esther, but then her gentleman friend told me she had died!"

He hung his head. "That's our fault, Mama. Tilly called Lou Ann and told her, but not until after they'd had the service."

"That sounds like Tilly. I'm surprised she thought to call at all. But why didn't you all tell me, for Heaven's sake?"

"Since you couldn't go to the service, we didn't see the sense of getting you upset right at Christmas. We planned to tell you afterward."

"Well, I guess we've both made a clumsy job of trying to protect each other from bad news, but at least we cared enough about one another to try."

"What?"

"Never mind that. How will we ever get down the mountain?"

"Don't you worry. I got that all covered. I put chains on my truck and I'm fixing to put some on your car. Lou Ann and you will drive home in your car, and I'll be right behind you in the truck."

"You all going to drop me off at the Methodist Home?"

"Now, Mama!"

"Terry Wayne?" she said when they had almost reached the door leading to the lobby.

"Yes, Mama?"

"Terry Wayne, I just can't stand it! If I don't tell you something, I think I'll just bust!"

"What's that, Mama?"

She stopped and looked him square in the face, her eyes on fire. She could feel it. "Terry Wayne, I think I've finally had it!"

He looked scared. "You've had what, Mama?"

"I've had an epiphany!" *A sudden manifestation of the essence or meaning of something; a comprehension or perception of reality by means of a sudden intuitive realization.*

She knew he thought she was crazy for sure now, but she had, she really had. Looking out the window a few minutes earlier, she'd seen something that had given her a small measure of peace and a sense, almost, of anticipation for what might await her around the curve of the tracks, beyond the next town and the next and the next.

"Well, Mama, I'm not sure I know what you're talking about," he said as they walked through the lobby, "but you seem happy about it, so I'm happy for you. I really am. There's snow at home too, you know, the prettiest snow I've ever seen, almost as deep as it is up here."

"You don't mean it! Down in Spindale? Well, I never would've thought it."

"Yeah, your hollies and nandinas are weighted down with it."

"Now *that* I want to see."

He helped her into her coat. The residents still up and about waved good-bye to her, them in those silly red caps.

"Just think about tomorrow, Mama," Terry Wayne said. "Tomorrow's Christmas Day. We'll build a big fire in the den, and make coffee and cocoa—"

"Oh, I can taste it now," she said.

"And we'll all be there, all your kids, all your grandkids, Bing Crosby singing 'White Christmas.'"

"And the refrigerator full of all that food I fixed. You all will have to eat it, too. Every last bit of it. You know I can't stand to think about food going to waste."

The thought of spending what might be her last Christmas with them all, well, that was about as close to the promised land as she needed to get for the time being. She'd kick up her heels and make it a doozy. *Seize the moment!* Jungle Buzzard had said. *Root hog or die!* Hobo Joe had said. Plenty of time to chase the moon after the first of the year. An eternity of shooting stars.

And she'd talk a blue streak when Elijah and Skye came to interview her again after the first of the year. She'd tell them all about the days between her years. She knew what she was talking about, as one of a generation who had looked out on its own brand of misery. She'd tell them it was a fine thing to do, to seek out those half-forgotten little stories about all the casualties that had never been counted, the casualties of things that might have been.

But she'd keep to herself what she'd just seen outside the window—the footprints in the snow from the edge of the woods to the window and back again, the deeper shadow in the shadow of the big spruce tree, the face of an old, old friend, the tip of a hat, the outstretched hand. She would keep it just like Mary had kept her own revelation. She would keep it, and she would ponder it in her heart.

Where the Woodbine Twines

A woman is confronted with an enigmatic figure from her past in this Southern Gothic thriller of unresolved friendship and unsettling memories. Set against the live-oak splendor of the South Carolina lowcountry and the dark glamour of Myrtle Beach in the 1950s, this tale of nostalgia, fear, and hope twists like a leaf in the wind.

ForeWord Magazine **2006 Book of the Year Award**
Honorable Mention / Fiction-General

"Extraordinarily fluent prose, subtle but telling character portrayal, an almost phantasmagoric episode at a carnival that Ray Bradbury could not have surpassed."

— S. T. Joshi, author of *The Modern Weird Tale*

"The elements of greatness."

— Rob Neufeld, *Asheville Citizen-Times*

"In this marvelous and mysterious novel, one unforgettable summer in a young girl's life becomes a cautionary tale for discerning truth and illusion, magic and metaphor. *Where the Woodbine Twines* is a haunting coming-of-age novel that will stay with you long after you turn the final page."

— Cassandra King, author of *The Same Sweet Girls*

"A strong and classy novella."

— Fred Chappell, author of *I Am One of You Forever*

"Austin's prose flows gently until the deeply running currents lure you into a dark and daunting place you're more than willing to go."

— Ann Patterson, *Spartanburg Herald-Journal*

ISBN 1-57072-315-X • $14.95

Mariah of the Spirits
and Other Southern Ghost Stories

Sherry Austin's first book takes you on a journey into the brooding, soulful American South where kudzu-covered hills hide dark family secrets, where souls rest uneasily under the soil of mountainside graveyards, old plantations are still haunted by a lost cause, and a phantom hitchhiker still walks on a moonlit coastal back road.

"Sherry Austin puts her fascination with the afterlife to effective fictional use in her debut collection, *Mariah of the Spirits and Other Southern Ghost Stories.*"
— *Publishers Weekly*

"The most frightening thing about this book would be if it were pigeonholed as just another collection of ghost stories, when these stories offer so much more than a good scare. What they offer is a well-lit glimpse into a dark and restless heritage."
— Wendi Berry, (Durham) *Herald-Sun*

"These poetic stories are firmly bound up in our culture, climate, and geography. . . . You'll recognize the vanishing hitchhiker, the unquiet grave, and other popular themes, but reworked in a fresh way that makes them seem everyday and oh-so-possible."
— Salem Macknee, *Charlotte Observer*

"Whether it's a curio shop in New Orleans or a North Carolina beach in autumn, Austin is an expert at evoking a sense of place where the supernatural seems, well, natural."
— Nancy Pate, *Orlando Sentinel*

"These well-told stories have both literary and creepy appeal as ghosts slink all over the South's gothic landscape."
— Hal Jacobs, *Atlanta Journal-Constitution*

ISBN 1-57072-315-X • $14.95

5/08